MAN ON A TRESTLE

BY KEN KENNEDY

Library of Congress Catalog Number 82-60483
International Standard Book Number 0-960-8864-0-0
Printed in the United States

Manufactured in the United States of America.

Screenplays by the author:

SILENT WITNESS
George Kennedy   Andrea Lane
Margie Reynolds   Bill Shanley
Triss Coffin

IRON ANGEL
Jim Davis   R. Wayland Williams
Margo Wood   L. Q. Jones
Don 'Red' Barry

VELVET TRAP
Thelma Davis   James Hurley

AGGIE
Thelma Davis   and guest
Nick Nolte

FATHER KINO STORY
Richard Egan   Ricardo Montalban
Michael Ansara   Joe Petrullo
Rory Calhoun   Aldo Ray
Joe Campanella   Cesar Romero
Anthony Caruso   John Russell
Triss Coffin   Keenan Wynn
William Dozier   Danny Zapien
John Ireland   Henry Brandon
Victor Jory   and special guest
Stephen McNally   Bishop Fulton J. Sheen

"It is a war of which the battlefield is men's minds. The minds of all men everywhere. And in which the weapons are the things by which men's minds are moved....words."

Archibald MacLeish

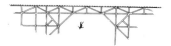

When Dr. Burton Cummins asked his office receptionist, Mary Parker, if she would accompany him on a weekend in Las Vegas, half his mind was hoping she would reject his pushful invitation, while the overworked amorous half of his mind envisioned her voluptuous body on a kingsized bed in a luxurious suite overlooking the Vegas Strip. Her long black hair fanned out in soft waves on a giant pink satin pillow, her arms held out to him invitingly, and later, the two of them making love in the billowing suds of a heart shaped Jacuzzi. His fantasy caused the blood to pound in his temples.

Mary Parker had several valid reasons why she should decline his offer. Dr. Cummins was a married man, and he had been married for more than the twenty-six years Mary had been alive. She also knew from experience that when an affair with a boss is over, so is the job. On the plus side, Burt Cummins was an attractive man who carried his fifty-eight years well. Mary Parker enjoyed sex and was, to her way of thinking, very selective when it came to bed-mates.

"Sounds like fun. I'd love to go," Mary had said.

Burt Cummins became absolutely giddy on hearing Mary's affirmative answer. He was Cervantes' Man of LaMancha, and he was about to reach his unreachable goal. The realization that in less than forty-eight hours he would no longer have to be satisfied with wondering and dreaming. Her tantalizing figure beneath those clinging knits would be his to have and to hold, to explore. No longer would he be bounded to a sneak look at her shapely legs and bottom when he would send her to return an empty manila folder to the fictitious "George Zimmer" file, which was in the lowest drawer of his personal file cabinet.

"You understand Miss Parker, we will have to be very....discreet," Cummins said bending close to her ear.

Mary nodded her agreement.

"Meet me here at the office Saturday morning, early?" Cummins asked. "The drive to Vegas is five hours."

"Or we could leave Friday night, if you can arrange it," Mary replied.

Burt Cummins felt the sudden flush to his face.

"Friday?" he managed to say. "Tomorrow night. Yes. Yes. We could take in another show."

"We could do that, too," Mary smiled.

That was the beginning, five months later the ending began.

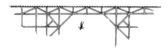

It was the second Sunday in April, and a warm afternoon sun slanted brightly on the Mexican border town of Tijuana casting an exact third of the downtown Plaza de Toros in deep shadow thereby creating a considerable difference in the cost of seats. Not that Dr. Cummins objected to the higher price of Sombra seating, but he preferred to sit among the more knowledgeable corrida spectators in the Sol section, and he would have done so this day if Mary Parker hadn't insisted on seats in the shade. Cummins did not attempt to explain Sol v. Sombra seating to a lady seeing her first live corida.

In fact, the doctor would have passed up this card of young, inexperienced fighters, if he had known the extent of their limitations, and if he had known what terror the next three days held for him, he never would have left Los Angeles. But, on their way to Phoenix Mary wanted to stop and see a ''Bullfight''. She had seen Tyrone Power and Rita Hayworth in BLOOD AND SAND on the LATE LATE SHOW, and nothing would do but she see the real thing.

It had been Mary's striking resemblance to Rita Hayworth that had first attracted Burt to her when she came to his office, supposedly in search of a job. Later, Cummins would learn that Mary's true reason for visiting a psychiatrist's office was to curb her sexual appetite. Once in the office, she became selfconscious, and, rather than admit her problem, she said she was seeking employment...as a secretary. Much to her amazement, Dr. Burt Cummins said, ''Can you start tomorrow morning, or later this afternoon? Perhaps we can go someplace for coffee and I can explain what your duties will be.''

Burt Cummins believed everyone deserves time to settle into a new office atmosphere, but after two weeks of retyping letters and correcting spelling, he was forced to hire another. The lady he found, (not nearly as attractive as Mary Parker and several years older) Joan, could do eighty words a minute and correct the dictionary. For Mary Parker, he created the position of office receptionist and file clerk; he just had to find something for her to do.

With some elation, Cummins remembered a morning last week. In answer to his usual greeting and "Any messages?", Mary had proudly reported, "A Mr. Professor Clark Hamilton from the University of California called and said that the papers he had written for you were ready and you could pick them up at his office, or, if you wished to have them sent over, just call him. His number is 943-8279." Then added, "Area code 213. I looked it up." As Cumming went back to his desk he thought, she's got it. By George, I think she's got it.

Burt Cummins considered himself somewhat of an aficionado. He had read Hemingway's DEATH IN THE AFTERNOON twice, Sidney Franklin's BULLFIGHTER FROM BROOKLYN and Barnaby Conrad's MATADOR. His Masters thesis in Psychology at Michigan included a section headed, "The Controlled Behavior of the Fiesta Brava."

His interest in the subject began in his grade school years due to a deep consternation regarding a phobia he could not understand nor diagnose in himself until he was in his third year of college. That was his "phobo-phobia." A fear of fear. And it would account for his strong preference for the term "Fiesta Brava" over Bullfight.

"A bullfight," Cummins often argued with classmates, "would consist of two bulls fighting each other. The proper title is Fiesta Brave...the pitting of man, not only against the horns of the bull, but against man's instinctive fear and his ability to control that fear." He admired courage in others and secretly abhorred the lack of it in himself.

In 1942 Burt Cummins was stationed at Fort Bliss, just east of El Paso, Texas. For eighteen months he was attached to the psychiatric section of the First Cavalry Medical Unit. Situated as he was on the Texas/Mexican border, he had the opportunity to study the Fiesta Brava firsthand. He attended more than two hundred coridas and saw over a thousand bulls dispatched. Many were brave kills; many more were butchery resulting from the fighters reluctance to move in over the horns for the kill.

Ironically, Capt. Burt Cummins was engaged weekdays at the base hospital in testing and separating the Section 8's from the genuine cowards. On Sunday afternoons Cummins crossed the Rio Grande into

4

the town of Juarez to watch the greats of the bullring: Procuna, Briones, El Salado and, of course, on special Sundays, the master, Carlos Arusa. Cummins used powerful binoculars to study each matador's face close up, the eyes, the tightening of the lips, the setting of the jaw before a particular dangerous pass or to detect any telltale sign that would divulge fear or even anxiety. What Cummins saw with this caliber of matador was disdain for the charge of the bull and complete confidence. For these fighters their kills brought cheers and "musica." The awarding of ears and tails was commonplace to these matadors, as was the single rough voice from the Sol section yelling, "HUEVOS GRANDE."

A roar came from the Sol section across the ring as the brass laden band played the first familiar notes of Augustin Laura's pasodoble, Novillero, a stirring musical tribute written for the young fighters of Mexico and most appropriate for the men who were about to display their skills before the judge and the many writers and photographers who lined the ring. Their reports and pictures, when published in Mexico City, would insure bigger and better fights for the man, if the review was laudable. If the writer and the photographer saw nerves and clumsy movement, that fighter would be selling his capes and swords for bus fare back home. And such a report, if heeded, might well save a fighter from an agonizing death in the ring. Still, there were those who so craved the recognition and riches attended the heroes of the bullring that they would rationalize a poor performance to such a degree of self-deception as to believe they had drawn a bad bull or there was too much wind. Another bull on another Sunday, in another ring, and they would be no less than fantastic. This driving egotism would eventually put a horn deep into their groin or rip the bowels from their cavity. Ring attendants would carry the fallen fighter to the infirmary under the stands. Bloody fingers intertwined attempting to hold unraveling intestines inside his cummerbund. His face would be contorted from pain and the realization that he would never face a bull again. Some of the crowd would be cheering the "brave" young man who was being hurried off to oblivion. Others would shake their heads and wonder aloud how he had gotten by so many horns without suffering a serious goring before this. Aficionados had little sympathy for those who would attempt to steal the 'musica.'

In the Patio de Caballos, behind the cuadrilla gates, men in brightly colored suits-of-lights were moving about adjusting their dress capes over the left shoulder and elbow. Four ring attendants vaulted the

5

barrera. They were dressed in the traditional tan pants, dark green shirts, dull red sash tied about their waist and dusty black caps with red visors. These were the young, still untried boys who had aspirations of someday fighting the bull, and the older men whose dreams had long ago been dashed in the sand but who had the sense to realize their limited talent in time. Yet, they, on occasion, would throw their bodies over a fallen matador to protect him from the charging horns. Cummins had seen this action on more than one Sunday and had written of it in his notes, "Impulsive reaction in the face of known danger to save the life of another." The young men hoped someday the gates of the cuadrillas would be opened for them, but on this afternoon they pushed the rough planking of the heavy gate to allow the Alguacil and his horse to enter the ring.

"The man on the horse is the president's deputy. He will accept the symbolic key to unlock the bullpens," Burt explained to Mary anticipating her question.

Music again filled the arena as the rider, dressed in the garbe of a sixteenth century nobelman, rode his black mount directly across the gray sand to the box of the president. Both horse and rider made a small bow, the horse digging an impatient hoof in the sand. Then the horseman removed his black plumed hat and held it high toward the president, and the president stood and returned the salute with a wave of a white handkerchief. Horse and rider then backed the full diameter of the bullring drawing a crescendo of wild applause.

The three novilleros, lined up across the open gateway, and the black horse, fighting nervously at the reins, once again entered the ring. The fighters followed with their stiff-legged and arrogant stride. Walking behind each fighter, purposely out of step, were the members of the cuadrilla. These were the more experienced men who would "run" the bull for the torrero and would often spot the bull in just the right position so the man could execute a particular pass. More important, these were the men who would draw the bull away from a fighter when he found himself in trouble or when he wished to disengage himself from the bull after a series of passes.

Many of the fighters place their own banderillas, the two foot long sticks wrapped tightly with bright colored paper, each stick having a sharp, fishhooklike, two inch steel barb on one end. If, for some reason, the fighter chose not to place his own "sticks", a member of his cuadrilla would perform that duty, too.

6

The act of placing the banderillas correctly was very important, and when executed incorrectly, which was often the case, it would ruin a bull's performance and thereby make the fighter look bad, too. The only men to ever attain true stardom in the bullring did all three acts perfectly and consistently. Cape, banderillas and a clean kill.

The three novilleros gained the far side of the ring just below Burt and Mary's seats on the barrera. The fighters removed their knobbed monteros, making sure the pinned-on pigtail of hair at the back of their heads was not disturbed, and acknowledged the plaudits of the crowd.

Mary Parker watched the spectacle unfold with growing excitement. The fighters were so close she could hear them speaking to each other in Spanish, which she did not understand. Then she blurted, "My God," and she leaned close to Cummins.

"Look at the buldge at their crotch," Mary said, "Is that real or are they hiding flashlights?"

"At least half is padding," Burt answered.

"Half would be plenty."

Mary tingled as she let her fingers do the walking up the inside of Burt's leg until her hand was hidden under the flap of his tan sport coat. Her hand was on him, but her mind was on them.

Cummins turned to study Mary's face. Her glistening tongue barely visible between her full red lips. Burt had seen that look many times in the past five months. He knew her power of voyeuristic fantasies and how real they became to her. Burt also knew that when they would be making love later that night in some motel between Tijuana and Phoenix, her needs would be fulfilled by the imaginative mastery of her carnalistic mind, which she defended by saying, "The sex drive in a woman is called 'nympho,' but in a man it is called 'macho.' Mary would have her bull-fighter, or fighters if she chose. What the hell, thought Burt, I will have Rita again.

The fighters were exchanging their sparkling paseo capes for the large working capes the attendants handed to them over the wooden barrera. They unfolded and spread the capes wide, and made a few exaggerated phantom passes, testing the wind. Burt wondered how much of their elegant style would vanish when El Toro appeared.

A lone trumpet, in counterpoint to the pasodoble being played by the band, sounded the call from high in the arena. The smaller gate marked "TOROS", swung open. Down the dark ramp from deep in the shadow of the pens came a three year old LaPunta bull. He ran, head high, into the blinding sunlight, straight across the ring, not swerving until his wide horns tested the far burladero palet. The crowd cheered. The Fiesta Brava had begun.

Having heard the trumpet call from inside the arena and the wild noise that always greets a good bull, the guards and helpers of the vast parking lot hurriedly moved into the entrance tunnels of the plaza. They, like the musicians, came to the fights every Sunday afternoon, not to work so much as to see the corrida in exchange for an hour of their time.

Near the center of the parking lot, two men, both Americans, were waiting in their car for the lot to clear. As they watched the last security guard walk into the tunnel, Robert Johnson, the man on the passenger side of the black Cadillac, said "Let's go." He opened his door and reached back for a brown paper sack on the seat between them.

"Anything else?" asked Karl Faber, the fat man seated behind the wheel.

"Bring the jack and the pry-bar," Johnson ordered, as he moved to the white 1983 Mark VI parked in the space directly in front of them.

The more than portly driver forced his stomach from under the steering wheel and reached into the back seat for the jack and the bar that had been flattened at one end to be used as a pry. He walked the few yards to where Johnson was standing by the left front wheel of the Lincoln.

"We got to jack this thing up?" complained Faber as he dropped the tools on the gravel.

"If someone should see us, we are just changing a tire."

Johnson crouched down with the brown paper bag, took the bar and placed the flat end between the hubcap and the wheel and removed the cap with the skill of a service station attendant. Placing the cap on the gravel, he took three green plastic bags from the paper sack.

"How can a small-timer like Hendricks expect to compete with the big syndicate boys?" Faber asked as he watched Johnson place the three plastic bags in the depression of the wheel.

"Don't sell Mr. Hendricks short," said Johnson reaching for the hubcap. "He has plans. Big plans."

"I know. This was one of them," said Faber.

"Besides his regular customers, in movies and in television, he's moving into professional sports." His voice reflecting his expectation of bigger things to come.

8

"So a few more jocks buy a packet..."

"You talk like a man with a paper asshold," said Johnson, as he punched the hubcap in place on the wheel. "The jocks Mr. Hendricks has lined up can control the point spread, even the winner of a game. Do you know how many millions go down on a Sunday? That's why these deliveries are so damn important."

"Those bags shift, they'll throw that damn wheel way out of balance," warned Faber.

"They won't be getting up to that kind of speed, just between here and the border," Johnson explained.

"Why don't we cut out all this bullshit and just put the bags under the seat and take them across ourselves?" Faber asked.

"You ever see the inside of a Mexican jail?" Johnson began. "They find this in our car and we would be thrown so far back in their rat infested dungeon no one would ever find us."

"If we have to blow this guy away like the last one, and we get caught, prisons up north aren't no damn country club."

Rising slowly, and looking to be sure they were not being watched, they stood up.

"Put these in the car," Johnson ordered, handing the tools to Faber. Johnson took a monocular from his pocket. He had borrowed this gadget from a friend of his who worked for the Pacific Electric Company. With this scope you can stand in an alley and read the tiny numbers on an electric meter a hundred feet away, but now it was being used to read the name and address on the registration card affixed to the steering column under the dash of the Mark VI.

"BURTON CUMMINS...3526 North Birch Street...Brentwood," Johnson was writing the information on the back of an envelope.

"What you writing?" Faber asked as he returned.

"This guy's name and address...just to be sure."

Faber and Johnson moved back to their car. They could hear the "Oles" and cheers from inside the bullring. The two men would seem, to any observer, to be American businessmen on a holiday in Mexico. A closer look at the deep scar on Faber's right cheek and the bulge under Johnson's coat might make one wonder just what type of business they were in.

Faber opened the driver's door and was struggling to fit himself beneath the steering wheel. Johnson reached over and hit the release rod and the steering wheel sprang up five inches, giving the driver more clearance than his ample waist required.

Faber settled himself behind the wheel.

"I always forget that damn thing," he said.

The roars of the crowd and the spirit of the music were a strong indication of the excitement they were missing within the arena.

"Aren't we gonna see any of the bullfight?" the driver complained.

"You get to see nothing but the ass-end of that Lincoln 'til we cross the border."

"Then what?"

"Then you force the car over, and while I check his tire you take care of him. Just like the others. Same deal."

Faber gave a frustrated look toward the multi-colored banners fluttering in the breeze from the poles that crowned the arena. "Why don't I ever get to do the hubcap thing?" Faber asked, still looking at the bullring.

"You enjoy what you do," said Johnson, "And, because I said so."

Faber pulled a beat-up copy of Penthouse from under the seat and quickly got his mind off the bullfight.

An uncurried team of brown and gray mules, with dirty red tassels dangling from their bridles and harnesses, was dragging the last bull of the afternoon from the arena. An aged muleteer, wearing a giant black sombrero, walked behind the dead animal. The long reins were held tightly in his left hand while his right flicked the rumps of the mules with a whip attached to a six foot rod. He carefully straddled the shallow furrow dug by the bull's left horn as it was pulled across the ring. Attendants in worn khaki pants and torn denim jackets were busy with wooden pegged rakes working the spilled blood into the sand and out of sight.

The people, those who hadn't departed after the work of the first picador, were making their way to the exits.

"Did you enjoy the Fiesta Brava as much as you did the movie?" Cummins asked Mary.

"Not the part with the horses," she answered. "Can't they do without the horses?"

"Not very well."

Walking the narrow passageway out of the arena, they were suddenly confronted by a smiling young Mexican boy not more than ten years old. His left arm encircled a bundle of banderillas, and his right hand held up two matching banderillas decorated with bright yellow and red crepe paper flowers at the center. These the small boy waved in Mary's face.

"Souvenier lady? Souvenier of bullfight? They got the blood of the bull on them," the youngster lied. "You buy, yes?"

"Oh Burt," said Mary as she accepted the colored sticks from the boy.

Burt reached into his pocket and drew out some bills and gave three, one dollar bills to the reaching hand. Taking the bills, the young bargain-driver held up four fingers and a beggar's smile. Burt had seen that smile in every bullring in Mexico, and not just from children. He gave the boy one more dollar knowing that if he had first offered four dollars he would be looking at five dirty fingers.

"Thank you, mister. You come back some day, see more bull-fights," and the boy turned away to other tourists.

Burt and Mary moved with the tide of people into the parking lot and walked directly to the white Mark VI. Two Mexican children with more banderillas approached them, but seeing the sticks Mary carried, they quickly took off for more fertile ground.

Mary was seated in the car. Burt had started the engine but had not put the car in gear.

"Couldn't we go backstage and meet the bullfighters?" Mary asked, as she touched the paper flowers on the sticks.

Burt knew she had been thinking about meeting the novilleros ever since the entrance parade and wondered why she had waited so long to ask.

"No, honey," Burt explained patiently. "The fighters are back at their hotel rooms by now, and they will be in the air flying back to Mexico City before we could get there." Then he added, "Put those banderillas on the floor in the back seat. They can be dangerous."

Mary turned and dropped the sticks over the back of her seat. As she did, Mary caught the eye of the fat man in the car behind them. She gave a small smile and settled back into her seat as the car moved with the flow of out-bound traffic.

The driver of the Caddy, watching from behind, turned to Johnson. "What's an old fart like that doing with a sweet young thing like that? I would show her what it's for."

"You couldn't make out in a women's prison with a handful of pardons. Besides, you get emotionally involved and you may not be able to do your job. Now get going and stay close behind him," Johnson ordered.

Cummins was moving the Mark VI smoothly into the slow trafic along the narrow streets of Tijuana, braking only for the pedestrians who dashed across the street in mid-block and for the candy and taco vendors who were moving against the direction of traffic with the hope of selling their wares to the passing tourists.

Darkness had fallen over the little town with the unseen setting of the sun. A single street lamp in the middle of the block gave a half light to the narrow, open front stalls that lined both sides of the street. Great patches of plaster had broken off and fallen away from exterior walls of the building exposing ancient rough adobe bricks whose mortar joints had eroded with time.

Dozens of paper pinatas in the crude form of pink chickens, brown and black donkeys and green bulls with red horns hung on a wire stretched over the entrance. Multi-colored serapes and sequin-trimmed sombreros were displayed. Leather belts and lady's purses piled high in boxes and on chairs spilled out onto the sidewalk. Standing on the curb, the clerks from the shops hawked their very special sale of silver bracelets and earrings.

The white Mark VI cleared a busy intersection where a tall, smiling policeman was directing traffic. The officer blew his whistle and raised his hand with an MP-like white glove and stepped in front of the black Caddy forcing a sudden stop.

"Why did you stop?" Johnson yelled.

"You want me to run over that guy? Look at the gun on his hip. The next size comes on wheels."

Other cars, heading for the border gate, were making right turns from the smaller side street and falling in behind the white Lincoln. Johnson was tapping his fingers nervously on the dash of the Caddy.

Another long blast on the whistle and the white gloves were waving the northbound cars through.

Many colored flags, high on their masts, were snapping in the strong evening breeze coming off the Pacific.

"That must be the border, where the flags are," said Mary. Burt didn't answer but kept moving to have his turn to tell the border inspector he had nothing to declare.

"I can't see the Lincoln. They must be five cars ahead of us," said Faber as he tried to see through the long line of cars.

"Keep going," Johnson urged. "We don't want to be stopped again. CAN'T YOU PASS?" His question had the loud, harsh tone of a command.

Faber responded by pressing the accelerator in an attempt to improve his position. At that moment one of the famous Tijuana taxis appeared out of nowhere, and that nowhere was an unseen alley. Faber hit his brakes and made a sharp lurch to the right knocking over a taco peddler's pushcart. Boiling grease from the cooking pot splashed into the man's face and soaked his torn khaki shirt front. He was screaming in pain and struggling to free himself from the broken spokes of the cart. People began running along the sidewalk to the accident.

"Back up." Johnson was yelling at Faber. "Go arond him. Hurry."

Faber backed the car the few feet of clearance he had behind him and then sped ahead. "Turn right, turn right." Johnson was frantic. "Take the first back street. Get to the border some other way. Move. Hurry."

"Good evening, folks," the border inspector greeted Burt and Mary. "What is your citizenship, please?"

"Both United States citizens," Cummins said, feeling proud in a way.

"Place of birth?" asked the inspector.

"Ravenna, Michigan," said Burt, and he turned to Mary.

Mary was leaning over Burt's lap to make eye contact with the inspector. "I was born in Los Angeles," she smiled.

"Anything to declare?"

"Just a pair of banderillas," Burt answered.

"Have a pleasant evening and drive carefully." The man leaned away from the window and looked to the next car. It was a Chevrolet.

As Burt said 'thank you,' he was moving up the highway to San Diego.

The tires of the black Caddy were screeching when they came around the last corner before the border gate. Two Mexican kids, selling Chicklets, were forced to jump out of the way of the speeding car.

From the curb, the kids yelled obscenities in Spanish that were far beyond their tender years. Roughly translated they said what should happen to the genitals of "gringos" who drive Cadillacs that hook to the right. The second boy yelled, "Your balls should be nailed to a stump, and you should be tipped over backwards."

"There it is," said Faber. "That's the border gate, but I don't see the Lincoln."

"Keep going."

The Cadillac came to a stop, a very bored inspector asked the question, "Citizenship?"

"American."

"Place of birth?"

"Toledo, Ohio," said Faber.

"New York City," said Johnson.

"Anything to declare?"

"No. Just came down to see the bullfights," said Faber.

"Have a pleasant evening, and drive carefully."

The Cadillac moved away slowly. "Move it, move it," Johnson was saying in a demanding whisper. "They are on the freeway by now."

"We'll catch em," said Faber. "They can't go over fifty-five."

"The hell you say."

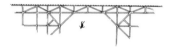

The mark VI was doing over sixty-five when it swung east at the intersection, away from the Los Angeles Freeway and circled onto Highway 8.

As they drove under the highway marker reading YUMA-PHOENIX, Burt Cummins said, "The car is steering funny. Might have a low tire. I'll check it first chance I get."

The young Texaco attendant applied his air gauge to the last of the four tires. "They are all up sir. I can take them off and check the balance if you want."

"No," said Burt. "It was probably the road or something. Those tires are less than two months old."

The attendant may have been listening to Cummins, but his eyes were following Mary as she walked with her special sway from the ladies room to the car.

"What's the damage?" Burt's voice brought the station attendant back.

"Twenty-two dollars, sir. Fifteen gallons."

Burt remembered to pay with cash. A few months ago he forgot and used his Gulf credit card on a clandestine trip to Las Vegas. When the bill arrived that month he had one hell of a time explaining thirty gallons of high-test gas and three nights for two at the Holiday Inn.

Mary was in the car when the attendant brought Burt's change.

"Twenty-two and three makes twenty-five."

"That's for you," Burt said refusing the change.

"Thank you, sir."

Burt turned and was reaching for the door handle.

"Sir," said the attendant, still looking into the car. "Is she a movie actress?"

"Sort of. She's a stunt woman." Then in a very confidential tone, "You might have seen her in DEEP THROAT or BEHIND THE GREEN DOOR."

Burt moved quickly into the car leaving the man nodding his head wondering and not really knowing just what he had heard.

"What was that?" Mary asked Burt as he started the car.

"Nothing. Just said drive carefully."

Burt was having his private joke, but it was true. Mary Parker could have been the stunt woman or the star of those films. Technical advisor for sure. Mary had taught Burt the art of oral love and made the lessons beautiful. Mary was a living, breathing aphrodisical lady. Burt's wife of twenty-nine years thought oral love was just "talking" about it. Poor Martha never seemed to get the hang of it, not even on those champagne induced nights. She, like any woman, had all the God-given equipment, lips, tongue, even teeth, but none of the talent that keeps the act from being crude, vulgar and downright painful. But he had God-given equipment, too. Five fingers on each hand, but he could not play Chop Sticks, not to mention Bach. And nothing sounds worse than Chop Sticks played badly.

The Lincoln was moving east on Interstate 8. The high-beam head-lights burrowed into the night. The digital clock on the dash displayed 9:05. They would arrive in Yuma near midnight - three hours. Burt looked over at Mary. She was asleep. Three hours. He would spend that time arranging his thoughts for the talk he was to give the next night, and he must remember to include the material Prof. Hamilton had supplied from his studies.

"Ladies and gentlemen," Cummins began his speech in his mind. "Tonight I would like to..." The front left tire was pounding hard and the vibration could be felt in the steering wheel. "What the hell is that?" Burt said aloud.

Mary looked up. "Do we have a flat?"

Burt made no answer. He pressed the brake pedal lightly, and when the car had reduced its speed to ten miles an hour he pulled off the highway and onto the gravel shoulder and stopped.

"Damn it." Burt said striking the steering wheel with his fist. "Hand me that flashlight from the glove compartment."

Mary opened the compartment on the dash and gave Burt the small, silver flashlight. "Everytime I see one of these I'm gonna think of those cute bullfighters," she giggled.

16

Burt took the flashlight and opened his door and moved to the left front wheel. In the beam of the light he could see the tire was not flat.

"Is it flat, Burt?"

"No, it's not flat."

"Maybe it's one of the other tires," Mary suggested.

Burt came back to the open window. "Push that little black button next to the glove compartment."

Mary pushed the silver button, and the tiny light in the compartment went out.

"The black one, next to that one," his voice became pained.

Mary pressed the black button which caused a metallic click at the rear of the car, and the trunk was unlocked.

Burt looked into the trunk. There was his brown leather briefcase, his gray zipper carry-all with his suits folded in the middle and Mary's powder blue make-up case and large matching suitcase. "Where the hell's the jack?" Danny Thomas flashed into his mind - Fifty-One Hundred Club, Chicago. He had laughed then. It wasn't funny now.

After rummaging around, he finally found the jack under the heavy carpet material that hung on the sides of the trunk. The jack and the wrench handle were all stored neatly in their rattleproof mounting. Burt pulled the jack from the elastic binding, and with the flashlight and jack he went to the front left wheel.

"Do you want me to get out?" Mary asked.

"No, you stay there. This won't take long. I'll put the spare on and see if it makes a difference."

A warm, April breeze was coming off the low desert, south of the Salton Sea, and Burt could feel perspiration building on his body. A faint, musty smell of irrigated land was noticeable in the air, but in the blackness of the night he could only see the circle of light coming from the flashlight.

Burt put the tools on the ground and placed a small rock under the lens of the flashlight so its beam was full on the tire freeing both hands for work. He picked up the jack handle and took the flat end and worked it between the rim and the hubcap. Two more moves and a little pressure and the cap was off. The light of the flashlight reflected on the three green plastic bags. Centrifugal force had welded the bags into a long narrow package at the bottom of the wheel.

"OH, SHIT."

"Did you hurt yourself, Burt?" Mary called.

"No, no. Nothing."

Cummins was mesmerized by the three plastic bags. He reached out and touched them with the tips of his fingers, his hand trembling. Burt knew what the bags contained the moment he saw them. Drugs. Many of his patients were being treated for drug addiction. There were the lectures and seminars he had attended with the Los Angeles police department and the many similar bags he had seen at drug busts. There was his brother-in-law in New Mexico.

Burt Cummins knew what was in the bags. The question driving into his brain with a sharp sting was, how did the bags get into the wheel, and why his wheel.

The answer to the first part was simple when you thought about it. His car was being used to transport the drugs across the United States border. The second part was tougher.

The perspiration was flowing freely now. His eyes burning, his breathing becoming heavy. Up the dark highway Burt saw the bright headlights and running lights of a semitruck. Those bastards with their damn CB's, he thought, they will radio the highway patrol and report a stalled motorist at mile post such-and-such. White Lincoln. California plates. May require assistance. Over and out, Good Buddy.

The eighteen-wheeler was still more than a mile up the road. Burt grabbed the three plastic bags, the jack, the handle and the flashlight and hurried to the rear of the car. He dropped everything onto the floor of the trunk and slammed the lid. Burt got behind the wheel and started the engine and spun his tires in the loose gravel getting up to speed and back on the highway.

"What's wrong, Burt?" Mary asked with alarm.

"Big truck. Big truck coming."

"Big truck?"

"Don't want to get side-swiped." Burt's fingers gripped the steering wheel tightly.

Mary turned in her seat and looked out the rear window.

The "big truck" was not gaining. Mary settled back into her seat. "Did you change the tire?"

"It's all fixed. No problem now." No problem, Burt thought. I have one hell of a problem, and I don't know what it is. I should stop right now and throw the stuff into the desert. His mind was racing. Those bags weren't put in that wheel as a gift. Someone had a plan to retrieve them. How? When? Burt was trying to clear his cluttered mind. "Whoever was going to get them back after I crossed the California line missed the connection,'' Burt was telling himself, ''and they will be coming after them. They will be looking for my car and their three plastic bags.'' Burt could feel his heart pumping and his pulse pounding at the back of his eyes.

Mary turned again and was looking out the rear window. ''I can't even see the truck now,'' she reported.

Burt looked down at the speedometer. He was doing over eighty. A cold chill went through him as he throttled back and set the cruise control at fifty-five.

''That's all I need - a speeding ticket,'' Burt was muttering to himself. ''Get pulled over here in the middle of nowhere. Smokey just loves to ticket expensive looking cars.''

In his mind's eye he could see the three, green plastic bags jostling about in the trunk of the car.

''It can't be marijuana,'' Cummins reasoned. ''It felt like powder in the bags. Cocaine. That's what it is. Pure cocaine. Three bags full. Yes sir, yes sir. Three bags full.'' His brain was speeding, and the fifty-five miles per hour he had slowed to was like walking. Before he had gone another mile he had made up his mind. ''That's what I'll do,'' he was telling himself. ''I'll throw the damn stuff into the river. When I get to the Colorado I'll stop on the bridge and throw the bags over the rail.''

Mary was asleep, and she could not hear Cummins debate with himself.

''If I stop on the bridge---no, I can't do that. Can't stop on the bridge. Takes too long to open the trunk, get the bags out and toss them over the railing. Someone would see me for sure.'' After a few moments, the proverbial ''idea bulb'' clicked on. ''I'll just go to the police, give them the three bags and then..., and then they will take our names, give the story to the newspapers, pictures...'' Burt drew a long breath. ''Think, just stop and think,'' he demanded of himself. ''Take it easy and think this thing out. I have three bags of coke back there. Maybe a pound or more each. That would be almost four pounds, in kilos that is...a kilo is a thousand grams. Street value is, say three million dollars. ''THREE MILLION DOLLARS?'' Burt could hear his own voice, but it was coming from somewhere else, from someone else.

''What did you say, Burt?'' Mary mumbled, still asleep.

Burt could not answer. He couldn't hold his hands on the steering wheel. He tried again to calm himself by taking several deep breaths. It didn't help.

"This isn't possible. It just isn't happening. It is happening. But not really, not what I think is happening. It's a joke. That's what it is, a joke, a sick joke. Those Mexican kids playing a joke on the dumb gringos. It's sugar in those plastic bags. That's it, just sugar." And for some dim reason, in the depths of his mind that thought was disappointing to him. "No," he finally said. "It's the real think." Then he sang, "Coke, It's The Real Thing."

Burt and Mary were now driving across the flat lands of lower California, through the giant sand dunes that stretch twenty miles west of Yuma, Arizona. In the distance Burt could see the lights of the city reflecting against the hazy night sky. Less than a half hour now to Yuma. The digital clock read 12:55. It would be 1:30 before he could find a motel. "Maybe I should keep driving," his lips were forming the silent words. "Gas up, get a cup of coffee and drive on to Phoenix."

At that moment his headlights reflected off a rectangular sign by the side of the road. The cat's eye letters jumped out at him: INSPECTION STATION AHEAD ALL CARS STOP.

"Shit." Burt hit the steering wheel with the heel of his hand. "I forgot about the damn inspection station. They will be checking for plants and fruit." Burt remembered the man always asked, "Any fresh fruit or any plants?" And you say, "No, sir," and he says, "Open your trunk, please."

Then a second sign: ONE HALF MILE - ALL CARS STOP.

Panic. Pure panic. "No one is going to believe my story." He was now on the bridge crossing the Colorado River. He was trapped. "Are the drug laws tougher in California or Arizona?" he was asking himself. "I'll turn off my lights and speed by." Then he remembered that every time he had passed one of these inspection stations they had a highway patrol car sitting there waiting for some dumb ass to try it. STOP ONE HUNDRED YARDS. Then Burt saw another sign. This one was orange with large black letters and an arrow pointing back onto the freeway. STATION CLOSED.

Burt's relief at seeing the station closed was as shaking as his fear had been of the inspection.

As he drove past the inspection office he could see it was empty. A large clock on the wall was back-lit. It read "Drink Dr. Pepper". The hands showed 2:00. Burt had forgotten the time change, too.

Yuma streets are never very busy during the day, and at 2:00 in the morning they are all but empty. A few truckers had parked along the curb in front of all-night diners. Some were working on their log book, or books, and some were getting their prescribed sleep time. Burt saw an orange ball of a 76 station. Puling into the driveway his wheels ran over a rubber signal hose that rang a loud bell. Mary woke at the sound as the car came to a stop.

"Where are we, honey?" she asked only half awake.

"Yuma."

Mary looked around, "So this is Yuma."

"With stopping for the tire and everything, we'll have to keep driving into Phoenix," Burt explained. "And I forgot about the time change. We lose an hour going east. Do you mind?"

"Okay with me, but I have to go to the little girl's room." Getting out of the car she asked, "Can we get some coffee?"

"Sure."

The service attendant came up to Burt's window. "Yes, sir, good morning."

"Good morning. Fill it up, please."

"Sure thing," said the attendant. Then, "Do you know you are missing a hub cap, mister?"

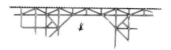

The newly painted white stucco on the two story home at 3527 Birch Street in Brentwood reflected the bright morning sun. A lush, green, well-manicured lawn undulated gently as it rose from the palm-lined street to the three-step, red brick semi-circle porch. Guarding the Georgian doorway were four Roman columns. Their ornate capitals supported a portico which extended from the second floor roof. A narrow, cement driveway curved past the home to a four-car garage at the rear.

Directly across the street from the Cummins home, Faber and Johnson waited in the Caddy. Haggard from their sleepless drive from Tijuana and all night vigil, they sat watching for the white Mark VI to back out of one of the four garage stalls.

Johnson was running a cordless electric shaver over his face. The fingers of his left hand were drumming on the car's mobile phone, a phone he might have to use within the hour to make a call he dreaded.

"Maybe you got the wrong address," suggested Faber looking up from his copy of HUSTLER.

"It's the right address," Johnson's tone matched his aggravation. He put the shaver in the glove compartment then checked his watch. "Nine thirty," he said. "I'm going up to the house."

Faber watched Johnson exit the car and walk with long strides across the street and up the driveway.

When Johnson pressed the doorbell, chimes were heard from inside. After a moment the heavy, paneled door opened inward and a gray-haired woman, wearing a black dress and neat, white apron looked out.

"Yes?" the woman questiond, "Can I help you?"

"Mr. Cummins. Is he home?"

"Dr. Cummins is out of town for a few days," the maid reported.

From back in the entrance-way a woman's voice called, "Who is it Corla?"

The maid turned from the door, still keeping a firm hold on the doorknob. "Someone to see the doctor, mam." Then she gave way to an attractive woman, perhaps in her late forties. Her make-up was most professional, and her light blond hair was brushed high on her head, the original color known only to her hairdresser or anyone taller than she. The other tell-tale problem were the age lines of her throat, and those she hid somewhat with the deft movements of her fluttering right hand as it flitted about her neck. The left hand held a tall glass of what might have been her breakfast tomato juice except for a short stalk of celery and the clinking of ice cubes.

"I'm Mrs. Cummins," she said, her voice rising.

"The lady said Mr. Cummins was out of town. Could you tell me where he is or when he will be back?" Johnson asked.

"Dr. Cummins should be back Tuesday or Wednesday," she said. "He is attending a convention in Phoenix."

"Phoenix?" It was the other side of the world as far as Johnson was concerned. "Is there some place I can call?"

"I might have a telephone number. One moment."

Martha Cummins was away from the door for only a few seconds when she called, "Here it is." Returning to the doorway with a small folder in her hand, she said, "They don't give a telephone number, but it is Mountain Shadows Hotel in Phoenix. And it is not a convention," Mrs. Cummins corrected herself. "It is the Southwestern States Seminar for the Study of Psychology and the Urban Society." Then looking at Johnson, "Dr. Cummins is the featured speaker," she said proudly.

Johnson extended his hand, "Can I see that?"

Martha Cummins handed the small, three panel pamphlet to Johnson which he folded and unfolded again to study the picture on the cover.

"Is this the doctor?" Johnson asked, indicating the picture.

"Yes, it is."

"Can I keep this?" he asked.

"Yes, you may." Mrs. Cummins' attempt to correct his grammar went unnoticed.

"Thank you, thank you very much." Johnson turned and hurried down the driveway.

"That Cummins guy is a shrink," Johnson said getting into the car.

"A what?" asked Faber.

"Cummins is a shrink, a psychiatrist, some big shot doctor."

"So?"

"So he's in Phoenix, Arizona."

Johnson studied the face of Dr. Cummins, smiling from the cover of the pamphlet. "Three hundred cars in that damn parking lot, and I pick this shit." He hit the picture with the back of his hand. The inevitable moment had arrived. Without looking at Faber he said. "Get the office on the phone."

It was 10:30 A.M., Arizona time, when the white Mark VI pulled off the Phoenix freeway and curved north going past Sky Harbor Airport, over the Salt River irrigation canal bridge, past the stone block entrance to the Arizona Biltmore and up 24th Street. When Cummins reached Lincoln Drive he turned east. His last visit to the "Valley of the Sun" had been three years ago. In those three years many changes had taken place. The large shopping center on the corner was open desert his last time by and so was the 18-hole golf course with its fairways roaming among giant Saguaros. One thing on Lincoln Drive had not changed, the ranch style home of Senator Barry Goldwater. The home set high on a knoll just south of the road with a directional antenna above the Goldwater "shack".

Cummins remembered the night he and his wife Martha had been awakened by the ringing of their bedroom telephone and the joyous surprise of hearing their son's voice.

"Hi Dad. It's me, Ron. Did I wake you?"

Their son Ronald was calling from somewhere in Vietnam. Martha Cummins was now fully awake and talking to her only child. Both Burt and Martha handed the phone back and forth as each thought of something new to ask.

When the call was completed Martha Cummins dropped her face into her trembling hands. Burt took their collie for a walk. It was to be the last time they would hear their son's voice. Three weeks after that call there was a telegam from the War Department. Pvt. First Class Ronald R. Cummins had died of wounds received when a land mine exploded beneath the jeep he was driving near the MLR. Burt looked with misty eyes at the antenna above the Goldwater "shack". It seemed to be searching the sky for other voices that were trying to tell us something. Burt wondered if we would listen this time. Burt Cummins had written to the Arizona Senator to thank him and to apologize for not voting for him.

Cummins turned off Lincoln Drive and into the entrance of the Mountain Shadows Hotel. He was suddenly jolted to the present. For a few moments he had been able to put the three plastic bags out of his mind, but now, in the driveway and parking area, he saw dozens of police cars all parked in trim rows with gold shields and silver stars on the doors and sparkling chrome visa-bars on their roofs which held sirens and red and yellow plastic housings for the lights. "What the hell is this?" Burt asked of no one in particular.

Mary looked out her window. "Sure are a lot of police cars."

Cummins pulled into the first empty parking space. He was telling Mary that he would leave the air-conditioning on while he checked in when a large figure blocked his window. The face of a hotel security guard was looking in the glass when Burt pressed the togle and the electric window came silently down.

"Good morning, sir," said the security guard. "You are parked in a Handicapped Zone. If you are checking in, will you please park in the Registration Zone by the front entrance."

"Sure," said Cummins, "sorry." And he backed the car out and pulled into the correct parking zone.

"Stay in the car and I'll get the key."

Cummins crossed the carpeted sidewalk and into the low ceilinged lobby. The contrast of the bright sun and the dimness of the lobby made seeing almost impossible. When his eyes became adjusted to the light he saw several groups of uniformed police standing about talking and laughing. Others, in golf and tennis clothes, were criss-crossing the lobby from desk to cocktail lounge. Cummins saw a large cloth sign that had been hung on the far wall. The tall black letters spelled 'WELCOME', but the tape holding the sign to the wall had given way at the upper right corner and had fallen half over itself. He could not read to whom the welcome was intended.

Burt Cummins moved across the lobby to the section of the desk marked 'RESERVATIONS-CHECK IN.' He waited for the lady clerk to put the last envelope in one of the tiny key boxes. She turned and smiled. "Good morning, sir, can I help you?"

"Cummins. Dr. Burt Cummins. I have a reservation."

"One moment please, Dr. Cummins."

The lady clerk flipped through the reservation file, "Dr. Burt Cummins," she read from the card. "Room 212." The clerk put a registration card on the desk and a ball point pen next to it. Cummins handed the girl his Master-Charge card. While Cummins was filling out the folio, the lady behind the desk had gotten his key, which she handed to the bellman who appeared at Burt's side.

"Thank you, Dr. Cummins, I hope you have an enjoyable stay." Indicating the bellman she said, "Carlos will show you to your room and help you with your luggage."

Carlos smiled and said, "This way sir...Your car is out front?"

"I'm parked in the registration zone."

On the sidewalk the bellman said, "I'll be right back...you will follow me to your room...you park in back."

Before Carlos could dash off to his electric golf cart with the fringe on top, Cummins asked, "What are all the police doing here? What's going on?"

"A convention or meeting of some kind. The sign in the lobby says, Welcome D.E.A., whatever that means." Carlos was running to his cart.

In the car Burt asked Mary, "Do you know what D.E.A. stands for?"

"D.E.A....? Beats the hell out of me."

"That's what I thought."

Carlos came by in his electric cart waving an arm as a signal for Cummins to follow him around the hotel to a parking section at the rear of Wing D.

The bellman steered the three wheel cart into the parking slot marked 213 and directed Cummins to pull into the space where the number on the curb read, 212. He stepped from his cart and hurried ahead to open the door and turn on the lights and the air conditioner.

Burt and Mary followed him into the room. Mary holding the gaily beribboned banderillas like a bride demurely carrying her nosegay. She placed the sticks on the low dresser against the wall.

The bellman then made his grand move of opening the heavy drapes to show the palm lined pool not twenty feet from their patio doors.

29

"Biggest hotel pool in the state." Then to Burt with his hand out, "If you will give me your keys, I will bring in your luggage."

"No, no. That won't be necessary...I will get them later." He handed Carlos two dollars.

"Thank you, sir," said the bellman, "The ice machine is just down the hall."

Burt closed the door and Mary walked to the glass patio doors. "He's right. That's the biggest swimming pool I ever saw. Can't wait to dive in."

"Pull the drapes, will you Mary. It will be cooler."

Mary slowly drew the drapes closed like the final curtain on some tragic play. When the daylight was shut out, Mary said, "Give me the keys and I'll bring my things in."

"I'll get them." Burt turned quickly and went out to the car.

As Burt put the key in the trunk lock he gave a quick look left and right, then lifted the trunk and took Mary's two cases. The three green plastic bags were in plain view. Burt closed the trunk and waited impatiently the few seconds for the automatic lock to take hold. He walked back to the room. Cummins put Mary's cases on the luggage stand at the foot of the king-size bed. The door to the bathroom opened and Mary stood in the door-way. She had wrapped a large white terry cloth bath towel around her and it was held by a small twist at the corners just above her full breasts. She was slowly brushing her shoulder length hair.

"Burt," Mary said thoughtfully, "Is anything wrong? Between us, I mean."

"No. Nothings wrong. What makes you ask a thing like that?"

Mary was lightly tapping the back of her hair brush into the palm of her hand. She moved over and sat on the edge of the bed. Her eyes were not on Cummins but instead she was looking down, busy with the truant hairs that had become entangled in the bristles. "I just have this feeling."

"Why should anything be wrong?"

"My being here with you for one thing...Vegas was for fun. This is business...maybe you are worried that I will embarrass you in some way...What if someone here at your meeting knows your wife? Maybe it would be better if I had my own room."

"That's ridiculous."

"Well, something is wrong. I don't know what it is, but there is something," Mary pouted.

"I don't know what you are talking about."

"All the way from San Diego...you never once tried to touch me."

"You were asleep."

"That never stopped you before."

"Come on, Mary.." Cummins was anxious to end the converstion.

"In Yuma.." she cut in. "Remember when we stopped for gas? I went into the ladies room. I took off my panties and put them in my purse, then I sat there in the car, waiting...and nothing. That's when I went to sleep."

Burt looked into her eyes for a moment. "Are they still in your purse?"

Mary rose slowly from the bed and her fingers untwisted the small knot at the corner of the towel and let it fall to the floor.

The three plastic bags could wait a little longer in the trunk of the car.

"Come here," Burt said, and they moved together.

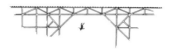

One half block off Cannon Drive in Beverly Hills, a two story building stands between two parking lots. To the north a fashionable Italian restaurant with a red, green and white striped awning above a red carpet running from the curb to the doorway. To the south is a popular beauty shop of the stars.

The center building's black marble veneer ran from the sidewalk to roof, alternating with narrow tinted glass windows giving the passing traffic a wavering reflection.

Over the double door a black iron rectangular sign, with raised gold letters read HENDRICKS & COOPER PUBLIC RELATIONS.

Pushing open the thick, glass door brought you into a large reception room. Your first reaction would be that you had entered a Hollywood portrait studio. On three walls hung giant black and white blow-ups of well known names in show business... none of which were clients of the company, but it did create the intended atmosphere.

An attractive blond was seated behind a U-shaped desk between two telephone consoles. The console on her left had seven incoming lines. The console on her right had three. Of the three, the red tab was flashing.

"Office." the blond answered.

"This is Johnson," the tired man in the Cadillac said. "Put me through, please, it's important."

"That line is on hold, Mr. Johnson. Mr. Hendricks is in a meeting and no calls are to be put through," and she hit the disconnect toggle.

Behind the receptionist was a no-handle door that was one of the large maple wall panels. Through this door you found a sizeable room with six desks, in two rows, each with a telephone and an IBM Selectric. The desks were separated by five foot high acoustical partitions which Baker Bros. had color coordinated to match the yellow, red and blue chairs and file cabinets.

Every week, from this office, more than five hundred aspiring actors and singers were advised to buy several dozen sets of 8 x 10 glossies and a demo record of their singing or a ten minute video tape of their acting talent. The hopeful novice is then guaranteed, orally, of course, that, with these tools in the hands of a good agent, their discovery by a TV producer or director was only a matter of time, and money. This was the front.

Below this office was a full basement and a sub-basement. The sub-basement had all the normal basement equipment, heating for both air and water, refrigeration for the building when needed and today it was needed. It was ninety and a smog alert.

The first basement was divided into sections by floor-to-ceiling chain link fencing. The smallest was the sign shop where paint and tons of poster cards were stored. The cards were now cut into various shapes and sizes, because on a demonstration the company had organized a year ago, a television newsman commented that all the signs in the demonstration were the same size and only two colors. "People don't seem to realize how much work and planning goes into a successful spontaneous demonstration," their spokesman explained.

In one corner were sheaves of five foot sticks to be used as standards to carry protest signs. Guns, staple and otherwise, were in the trunks of the workers cars. That was standard.

The remainder of the basement was storage for folding chairs, bullhorns, motion-picture projectors, screens and public address systems and podiums.

The heart of the operation was the second floor which had it's own private entrance from the rear parking lot, or directly from the basement by way of a small clanky elevator.

It was on this, the second floor, the uninterruptible meeting was being conducted. The room was the largest in the building and easily accommodated the seven bridge tables now placed in a circle. Mr. Hendricks insisted on this seating arrangement so he would have eye contact with each person at all times.

Along three sides of the room were leather couches and oxblood wing-chairs. Small coffee tables fronted each couch. On a glass-top table, near the room's only door, was a silver Samovar from which hot tea would be served at meeting intermissions.

When Hendricks held classes for indoctrination of new recruits, using film and slide presentations, folding chairs would be brought from the basement and set up theatre style to accommodate sixty.

On this day, Hendricks was, as usual, conducting the meeting and as usual the meeting droned into a self-serving lecture.

The desk at which Hendricks sat was large and studious. It had been bought from a Hollywood prop department when the company went under. The last time the desk had been seen on the screen Edward Arnold was seated behind it, playing a big-time politician and his wonderful laugh bounced off the polished top. The man who sat there now had never been known to laugh, and only on rare occasions to smile.

On the wall behind Hendricks' desk was a large sign:

PROPAGANDA NOT FOLLOWED WITH ACTION

IS WORTHLESS

Hendricks was saying… "always remember that ours is a service. A service that forms and presents ideas. A service that introduces ideas to the media. Here they will be printed and spoken around the world. We must supply the ideas to the media people in such a way that they firmly believe the idea originated in their own minds. Those wonderful malleable American minds."

The four men and three women were making notes on the small white pads in front of them.

"We must at all times deal in truth," Hendricks cautioned. "Truth that is easily authenticated." Their leader leaned forward over his desk. "It is the slant of that truth which we supply." The words were followed with a knowing look at each listener.

Hendricks relaxed in his chair and removed his steel-rimmed glasses and began cleaning them. An unnecessary action done only for effect and to give his people time to make notes. His eyes were beady when not seen through the thick lenses. His black beard rounded each cheek and met under the chin and he had no hair on his upper lip and less on his head. His white shirt was a tinge lighter than his skin and in sharp contrast to the black of his beard, suit and tie.

When he thought he had given his people sufficient time to digest his words, he held his glasses at arm's length and examined them against the ceiling or fluorescent lamps. Then he drew the attention of his listeners to the large sign on the wall to his left.

OUR GOAL IS VICTORY IN THE ARENA OF IDEAS

NOT THE BATTLEFIELD

Hendricks was putting his glasses back on when his secretary came up behind him and placed a note on the top of his desk.

"He has called four times in the last fifteen minutes" she said softly.

Rising from his chair, Hendricks looked at the seven people, "I'll only be a moment."

He left the meeting room and went directly to his office. The center phone on his desk was flashing. Leaning over the desk he jerked up the receiver. "Where the hell are you?

"We had a little trouble at the border," Johnson was saying. "We fixed the wheel . . . but it got away from us."

"It got away? Two million dollars of my merchandise got away?"

"I know who has it . . . I went to his home . . . it's not there."

"I'm already two weeks late for distribution . . . Where the hell is it?"

"Phoenix."

"Phoenix?" Hendricks yelled into the phone, "Where in Phoenix?"

"Mountain Shadows Hotel. Name's Cummins. He'll be there for two or three days. When he comes home, we will be waiting for him."

"Wait, shit." Hendricks pounded a fist on the top of the desk. "You be on the next plane to Phoenix. You find my merchandise and you bring it back here, do you understand?"

Hendricks moved around his desk and sat down. "Now you listen. Pick up your tickets at Western Airlines. They will be in the company name. I have people working in Phoenix on the Palo Verde nuclear project. They will deliver a car to you at the Phoenix Airport. You will meet at the Western Airlines baggage carousel and don't take a chance on the airport detectors, use the tools you will find in the trunk of the car."

"Got it."

"And Johnson... If you miss this time...they might just bury you in the Arizona desert."

"I'll get your merchandise and fly back tomorrow."

"You don't fly back, you drive back. How soon can you be at the Airport? Where are you calling from?"

"I'm on the car radio…"

"You are on the radio?" His voice was getting louder with each word, then… "You shithead," and he slammed the phone down onto its cradle.

After a moment Hendricks reached into the bottom drawer of his desk and brought out a half-filled bottle of Stolichanaya. Not finding a glass he took a long drink from the bottle. "If I lose one contact because of their stupidity…" Hendricks put the bottle back in the drawer and on his way back to the meeting room, advised his secretary, Mrs. Cooper, to make all arrangements at Western Airlines and to call the project leader in Phoenix.

Back in the meeting room, Hendricks waited for the circle of people to come to classroom order. When he had their full attention, he began, "Each of you has been doing a wonderful job over the past year. Wonderful. Each department is making great headway. Our clients are pleased beyond words. Your people in Section 'J'," he addressed the lady at the second table to his right, "your inroads in the youth movements, the recording business, the acceptive condition to alcohol and narcotics has been remarkable. We knew we would attract the twenty year olds, but eleven. Great job."

The leader of Section "J" was doodling on the pad before her. Then she took her pencil and ran it through the twisted bun of her hair, worn high on her head. "I, too, was surprised to find more kids turning onto grass than tobacco, thanks to the Surgeon General and his 'Cigarette Smoking Is Dangerous To Your Health.' At least that is the way it is in the classes I teach."

Hendricks was addressing the seven now, "We must remember that what we are doing, our combined effort is only the foundation. This will, of itself, create a void. The parents will say, 'No, don't do this or that,' the school and their peers will say, 'Yes, go ahead, do it,' this after a time will break down the 'family' authority, a small thing in itself, but it creates that void. Then into that void we insert more suspicion and doubt. As the void widens we add fear and mistrust in their leaders in government at all levels. From the stupid school board, through the bungling city councils, and up through state and federal governments. Fascinating how quickly the defiance of authority grows." Then he smiled, "You saw the president's daughter at last month's demonstration, I'm sure."

Hendricks turned a few sheets of typewritten papers over on his desk and scribbled a note to himself across one and began speaking before looking up to his people.

"Mr. Clark has some interesting thoughts on our overall program," Hendricks then moved his hand toward Mr. Clark who was seated across the circle.

When given the invitation to address the meeting, Clark shifted in his chair, cleared his throat and removed his glasses.

"For the past six months," Clark began, "I have been concentrating on the target of our overall operation, the underlying main target. What were our final goals, and how best to achieve them within the limits of our guidelines, and which of our operations were the most productive?" He leaned forward, his elbows on the table and his glasses held between his hands in a prayerful attitude. "Four years ago, I don't know who first said it, but the term 'gas guzzler' hit the news wire and became an adjective in the lexicon of the environmentalists. It was picked up and printed and broadcast in all media. Gas-guzzler then took on the form of a synonym. Whenever the news referred to one of the large American built automobiles, no matter what the make, they labeled it a 'gas guzzler.' It made the driver of a big car, un-American. The true patriot would buy and drive a small compact car to do his part to conserve energy and protect the delicate balance of the environment. But where would he find the small, compact car? Not in Detroit, that's for sure." Everyone in the circle smiled in agreement. "Several years ago," Clark went on, "America had the little Crosley, it delivered sixty miles to the gallon, then the Henry J. It was a little bigger and still did thirty to thirty-five miles per galon. We were worried for a short while that even the small Rambler would become popular. But just driving small cars was not our scheme, and for a while it was touch and go. Our campaign then was to point out the danger of the small car and how your chances of surviving, even a minor accident, were almost impossible. After these cars left the scene, the American people quickly forgot the admonition of the danger in the small car, and when we hit 'gas guzzler' and 'Detroit Iron,' it worked, and is still working. As you can see, the automobile industry in this country is in shambles. Factories are closing, and thousands of American people are out of work. We are at last slowing down the wealth generating machinery of America.

"The prime objective of our client's multi-billion dollar missile arsenal is an eventual strike at the industrial heart of this country, and a crippling strike or series of strikes at the vital industries. We have nearly destroyed America's largest, most important industry, the manufacturing of their automobiles. The shock wave that will later hit the periphery of the industry, the smaller feeder companies, will be economically devastating.

"By cutting off the head of the serpent, the American car, the countless suppliers will only wiggle till sundown, so to speak. Steel, mines and smelters, copper, tire makers, wire and bearings, the list goes on.

"Our client won't need his missiles to do the job.

"And the wonderful part is, we are letting the American people do it to themselves."

Hendricks gave a slight cough, a signal to Mr. Martin to end his report.

"Thank you Kevin," Hendricks said while looking at his notes. "The final subject to cover for this meeting is a new acquisition for us, but of equal importance to us. This is our continuing opposition to atomic weapons with particular attention to the curtailment of nuclear energy. And, even after the short time we have been active on this project, we see it is beginning to pay off, and at the rate of fifty million barrels of oil a day the United States must purchase from our clients. And our well-meaning environmentalist friends are doing a magnificent job for us. Professor Hamilton will give us that report."

Hendricks swung his chair to the left to introduce Professor George Hamilton.

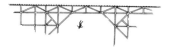

Burt Cummins stood by the half open bathroom door of their hotel room listening to the water storming against the opaque shower curtain, and Mary's voice as she sang her acappella arrangement of "HOLD ME BABY, HOLD ME". Steam had filled the small tiled room and clouded the mirrors above the twin sinks. A few times, while soaping her legs and back, Mary had pressed lightly against the shower curtain and a very attractive portion of her body could be discerned, like looking at a face through a frosted window in winter. And when Mary dropped her bar of Dial and bent to pick it up, it was a new angle of 'Spring Morn.'

Burt had to force back desire and remember he was on his way to take care of important business, the three green plastic bags in the trunk of his car.

"Mary," he called, trying to be heard above the shower and her song. "I'm going to bring my things from the car."

There was no answer. Mary was starting her fourth chorus and Burt hurried to button his shirt.

Cummins moved out of the hotel room toward his car and, while walking, he drew a ring of keys from his pocket. As he separated the trunk key from the others, his mind once again began building the frightening anguish Mary's body had held in abeyance for the last hour, but now the fears were once again mounting.

"The only sane thing to do is dump the stuff down the toilet," Burt was telling himself. "Get rid of it. Forget the whole thing." But the nagging inglorious shadow lurking in some hidden crevice of his brain, labeled 'greed,' prevented the action of flushing two million dollars.

"How the hell does one turn narcotics into money anyway? You have to have someone with connections. Like in the movies and on television. The guys in the pin-striped suits and dark glasses. The connection. Without a connection there is nothing. You can't run a damn ad in the paper. FOR SALE Three bags pure cocain. Best Offer Takes All Call.... You are in or you are out and I am out. So down the sewer. Down the sewer with all the other shit. I never asked for this stuff. It's not like I had a huge investment to protect. To hell with it. When the guys come looking for the stuff I'll just tell them I don't know what they are talking about. Or I didn't know what it was and I flushed it down the toilet. Or, the hubcap came off and it was strewn all over the freeway. That's what I'll tell them...and they will put a bullet right between my eyes."

The turn of the key in the electric lock made a loud 'click' as the trunk opened and the bright sun danced on the green plastic. Cummins leaned fully into the trunk, covering the three bags with his body. He pulled out his briefcase that had become wedged between his suitcase and canvas carryall. His nervous fingers seemed to tangle as he manipulated the brass wheels of the combination lock. When the case finally opened, Burt quickly tossed its contents onto the floor of the trunk. Papers, notebooks, pens and pencils, pocket recorder, magazines and four sheets of typewritten pages. These were the research findings sent to his office by Professor George Hamilton.

Burt placed the three plastic bags in the briefcase and closed the cover. As he spun the combination wheels...

"Sure gonna be a scorcher," said a voice not more than a foot from Burt's ear, or so it seemed. Burt was so startled he hit his head on the trunk cover. Still, he held the handle of his briefcase tightly in his right hand, and there was a sudden constriction of his throat.

At the rear of the car parked to his left he saw a man, pehaps in his forties, a full head of red hair and a walrus mustache to match. The man was dressed in a loud yelow and green checked pair of slacks and a solid yellow golf shirt. Burt had not heard the man come up or open his trunk which was not more than five feet away and he wondered how long he had been there and how much he had seen. The redhead was lifting his heavy leather golf bag into the trunk of his car and then leaned in and brought out a pair of black loafers and dropped them on the ground by his feet. Burt watched as the man turned and sat on the edge of the open trunk and began taking off his spiked golf shoes.

"Must be near ninety," Burt finally said while looking up to a blinding sun.

"Hell, it was ninety-two when we turned the back nine."

"Getting hot early this year," Burt's breathing was almost under control. Then, just to make conversation, "Our last meeting was in July. I don't know why they pick Arizona in July."

"Half price, that's why." The man was trying to flip his shoe over with the big toe of his left foot. "We have two meetings here a year," he managed to get his foot into his loafer, "every other one is hot as hell."

Burt shifted the briefcase to his left hand and extended his right. "I'm Burt Cummins, I'm from Los Angeles."

The two men shook hands. "I'm here with the Western States Psychiatrists Seminar," Burt offered.

"Vince Reed," the man's grip indicated his potential strength. "I'm here with the D.E.A."

"I saw the banner in the lobby. Pardon my ignorance but, what is the D.E.A?"

"Drug Enforcement Agency," the man said simply.

It was like a baseball bat right across the bridge of the nose and the redhead smiled when he said it, sort of an, "I got'cha" smile.

"I'm from San Francisco," the man went on, "but I work out of Washington now, and believe me, a hundred and five here isn't as bad as eighty-five there."

Burt Cummins was standing face to face with a policeman, a drug enforcement policeman. The first one he had ever met in his life and it had to be here, now, today, standing with a briefcase whose contents could send him to prison for life, or longer. The lump was reforming in his throat and if he didn't speak now he may not be able to ever again. "What does the D.E.A. do?" he managed to say, sounding like a drowning man gasping for air.

"Mostly we try to find where illegal drugs are coming from, how they are being transported. If it's by air, or by boat, truck or car. Whatever. One guy in L.A. was making shipments by United Parcel for months. Did a hell of a business, till one day a package broke open, and that was the end of that. We don't stop all of 'em but we keep trying."

"Dangerous work?" asked Burt.

"Occasionally, but mostly for them."

"Them?"

"They fight among themselves. Somebody tries to rip off a delivery and someone gets killed. Happens all the time."

"It does?"

"When you are playing with that kind of money, some people will take a lot of dumb chances."

"They must be dumb all right." Burt was giving an agreeing nod.

The D.E.A. man gave a friendly smile, "Have a nice day." Then he closed the trunk of his car and moved across the parking lot.

Burt waited and watched the man in the wild yellow golf outfit walk away, he then turned to see that the trunk of his car was still open. It was easy to see the disarray of papers and things, and if the D.E.A. man had seen the plastic bags, even for a split second, he would have known what they contained. Burt knew what they held in two seconds, a trained narcotics agent would know instantly. But he hadn't given a hint, only that knowing smile.

Burt took his shaving kit, closed the trunk.

Mary had finished her shower and was standing before the bathroom mirror drying her hair with an electric blow-dryer. She had again wrapped a large terry cloth towel around herself with a small twist knot secure under her arm. Burt came up behind her and forced a smile at Mary's reflection in the mirror. As he reached around her to place his shaving kit on the marble top sink he kissed her neck lightly and she feigned a thrill and playfully brought the dryer up to her shoulder so the rush of hot air was full in his face. For a split second, as the hot air forced his eyes closed, Burt wondered if this dryer was one of the asbstos type that cause cancer. Then he was thinking of a friend whom he had convinced, over a period of months, that cigarette smoking was dangerous to his health. The friend quit smoking and two years later died from cancer of the colon. He did not pursue the thought.

"Do you want to get in here?" Mary asked.

"No, you finish while I make a phone call."

The telephone was on a small round table next to the patio windows. On each side of the table was a high-back Nagahyde chair. Burt pulled the phone forward to make a space for the briefcase, turned and sat down heavily. He placed the phone on his lap, took a very deep breath and exhaled slowly. This was an exercise to calm the nerves which he had given to his patients many times. He hoped it had done better for them than it was doing for him now. Burt lifted the receiver and pressed nine. When he could hear the tone he dialed his home number. While the number was ringing, Mary came into the room and sat in the chair across from Burt. He held a finger to his lips and Mary gave an understanding nod.

"Hello." It was Burt's wife Martha who answered the phone and he had expected Corla the maid.

"Hi, it's me," Burt said flatly.

"Oh, Burt dear. I'm glad you called. Did you have a good trip?

"It is hot."

"I waited up for your call last night," there was disappointment in her tone.

"I had tire trouble on the way and it was very late when I got in, and with the time difference... I didn't want to wake you."

"I was awake."

"Where is Corla? How come you answered the phone?"

"Corla is busy fixing a Bloody Mary for me, if you must know," Martha Cummins giggled lightly and Burt knew it wasn't her first of the day.

"Were there any calls?" Burt asked.

"Yes, there was. A man came by about an hour ago. He said he wanted to see you. Some business or something. Said it was urgent."

"He did?"

Mary looked up sensing Burt's consternation.

"The man asked where he could reach you," Mrs. Cummins went on, "I told him you were at the Mountain Shadows Hotel in Phoenix."

"You did."

"Must be important. He even asked for your picture."

"My picture?" Burt sat forward in his chair.

"Just that little pamphlet about the meeting with your picture on the cover."

"You gave my picture to a stranger and told him where I was staying?" Irritation mixed with fear was in his voice.

"He knew where you lived," his wife continued. "Is something wrong?"

"Nothing is wrong," said Burt, not wanting to worry his wife unnecessarily. When Martha worried she needed something to settle her nerves. Lately she had been practicing preventive medicine up to a pint a day. "Whoever it is I'll see him when I get home."

Before his wife could say anything, Burt cut in, "I'm late for a meeting now so I have to run. I'll call this evening."

Mrs. Cummins was still talking as Burt put the phone back on its cradle.

"He's on his way," Burt said softly.

Mary moved from her chair and knelt before him, laced her fingers over his knee and asked, "Who is on his way? What is it, Burt? What's the matter?"

Burt gave no answer. He didn't even look at Mary. His head was back on the chair and his eyes were closed, his face grimacing.

"I know something is wrong," Mary insisted. "Please tell me what it is. Maybe I can help." Mary waited, still no answer, then, "Is it me? Do you want me to fly back to L.A.? It's all right, I understand. I'll be at the office when you return. Please tell me. Please."

"Mary, it has nothing to do with you. Nothing at all. In fact, it doesn't have anything to do with me. At least it shouldn't."

"I don't understand, but I want to help if I can."

Burt waited a long time then placed the phone back on the table and took the briefcase and placed it on his lap.

"Mary," Burt began, "I don't want to get you or anyone else involved in this. It wouldn't be safe for you."

"Safe for me? What the hell is going on?"

Burt's fingers played with the brass combination wheels on the lock of the briefcase. "All right," he said. "I'll tell you as much as I can, then I'm going to put you on the first plane back to Los Angeles."

"Burt, for God's sake, what is it?" Mary was in tears. "I'm not leaving if you are in some kind of trouble."

"Let me tell you what has happened, then you'll understand why you must go back, why it's not safe for you here."

Mary made an attempt to speak.

"While we were watching the bulls yesterday, someone put these in the hubcap of my car." Burt spun the last wheel of the combination lock and opened the latch. Slowly he raised the cover and Mary could see the three green plastic bags. "I think these bags contain pure cocaine."

"OH, MY GOD." Mary was on her knees before Burt looking into the case. She reached out and touched the bags with the tips of her fingers, not sure if what she saw was real. "Why in your car?" Mary asked without her eyes leaving the three plastic bags.

"Maybe they got the wrong car, or maybe they were going to stop me when I had crossed the border and get it back. Anyway, they know who I am, and they know where I live. They could have gotten that from the license plates, but now, thanks to my wife, they know I'm staying at this hotel. They even have a Goddamn picture of me."

"Are you sure it is cocaine?" Mary asked.

46

"I'm sure."

"I've never seen that much before. Must be worth thousands."

"Millions."

"Millions?" gasped Mary as a glaze came into her eyes and her fingers once again trailed lightly over the green plactic bags. "Millions," she repeated. Suddenly dazzling skyrockets were exploding in her mind. Each sparklking burst of multi-colored flames framed a dream more extravagant than any list of gifts to ever tantalize a daytime television game-show contestant. Mary had passed jewels and furs and was starting on palatial mansions and sleek yachts, when Burt's voice extinguished her pyrotechnics.

"Might as well be worthless as sand."

"Worthless?" Mary was trying to hold on to her dream.

"To turn this into cash would take connections. A pusher. I want no part of that." Burt closed the briefcase and spun the combination lock with a protective and possessive manner. "All I know is that they are coming for this stuff and they will be asking or shooting. That is why I want you away from this. Somewhere safe till this is over."

There was a long pause. Neither spoke. An abandonment of a dream, an hallucination to which they had both become addicted. It was Mary who broke the silence.

"They, whoever they are, know you are at this hotel. Why not leave the briefcase at the front desk, and when they come asking for you, have the clerk give the case to them?"

Burt was unconsciously rubbing small circles with the palm of his hand over the soft brown cover of the case. "I know it is ridiculously insane, but I can't just throw away an opportunity like this."

"Opportunity to get yourself killed."

"There must be a way."

Mary rose from her knees and walked to the far side of the room. Then, turned suddenly.

"You say the problem is finding a buyer? Well, whoever put those bags in your car, he's your buyer." Mary looked at Burt for some reaction, then, "If the stuff is worth what you say, they will want it back and they will pay for it. Sort of a reward."

"Reward," Burt repeated the word slowly and thoughtfully. "A moment ago you said you had never seen 'that much' before. You have seen cocaine before? You don't use it for God's sake?"

"No, I don't use it," Mary explained. "A disco joint I go to on the strip, a lot of it is floating around. Some big names on it, and they make no attempt to hide it. Most I ever saw was a little pinch," Mary held her thumb and forefinger together. "Just that much they said was a hundred dollars."

"It's not cheap."

"It's not worth getting your head blown off for either."

Burt rose from his chair and walked a few steps to the center of the room, holding the briefcase in his arms.

"Reward," he repeated. "It might work, and it sounds so much better than ransom."

"Burt, I'm sorry. It was a crazy idea. Leave the case at the front desk and let them pick it up."

"Let me think."

"If it would make you feel better, you could tip off the police and they can nab whoever it is when they come to get the stuff." Mary suggested.

"All they want is the cocaine." Burt went on. "If I bring the police into this, and they do catch whoever they are, others of their organization will be after me. The reward idea. It's the only way. No others get involved who aren't already involved, but we have to have a plan."

"We?'

"The reward was your idea, wasn't it?"

"Yes, but..."

"What time is it?"

Mary reached over and looked at his wristwatch, "Five after twelve."

"That's five after one here. That man was at my home three hours ago. It takes seven to eight hours to drive to Phoenix."

"Or one hour to fly."

"Hurry and get dressed. We have to find some place to hide this briefcase."

"Hide the briefcase?"

"Just hurry."

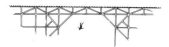

At exactly 1:05 PM, Western Airlines flight 312 touched down at Phoenix Sky Harbor Airport.

Pamela Cook was standing on the enclosed observation platform overlooking the twin runways. As the wheels of the Boeing 727 made contact with the concrete, the tires trailed a thin blue wisp of smoke, but the familiar screech of rubber could not be heard through the heavy plate glass wall. Nor could Pamela Cook hear the powerful roar of the jet engines as thy reversed thrust to slow the plane's momentum. The girl gave a quick glance at her wristwatch. "Right on time." That was important to her.

Pamela was twenty-three years old, medium height. Her tight fitting jeans and high heel boots gave the imprssion of a much taller and stronger girl. Long chestnut hair drawn about her oval face and gathered at the nape with a silver barrette. The oversized Foster-Grants, gave her a studious appearance which was entirely cosmetic.

The telephone call from Hendricks that morning allowed her two hours to prepare a car with all the necessary papers and maps, and have it ready and waiting in the terminal parking area by one o'clock, which she had done with seven minutes to spare.

Pamela Cook prided herself for the talent of setting a schedule and keeping to it.

She had not only completed all the arrangements that had been ordered from California in the allowed time, but she had included an important telephone call to a local television station for her own project.

When her call had been transferred to the news room, she asked:
"Could I speak with the assignment editor, please?"

"This is the assignment editor," a male voice answered.

"I'm calling regarding a very important and newsworthy event that will take place this coming Friday afternoon at one o'clock." Pamela Cook was using her best PR voice.

"Yes," was the bored reply.

"At one o'clock on Friday more than two hundred concerned citizens from all parts of this state will join to form a wall of defiance across the entrance to the nuclear generating plant west of Phoenix," her voice becoming more dramatic.

"What organization is this?" asked the newsman. "We are not a true 'organization,' sir. We are only concerned citizens trying to avoid another Three Mile Island."

"And two hundred people are going to just happen to drop by the plant on Friday to form this human wall?"

"To that extent we are organized. We have notified the newspapers in the Valley and there will be other TV news people there, too."

"Well, lady," the assignment editor said, "looking at our assignment board, I see Friday mid-day is really jammed up. I couldn't possibly have a camera crew out there till after three. That plant is sixty miles out in the desert."

"That will be all right. We can have the demonstration shortly after three. We want to give you time to make the six o'clock news."

"We appreciate your thoughtfulness." Pamela Cook did not recognizee facetiousness when she heard it. "I won't guarantee anything. Perhaps you should send a letter to the station with all the details."

"Thank you, I'll do that. And is there a chance that you can feed this story to the network?"

"That depends."

"It will really be something. Great visuals. Not a lot of talking heads." She proudly inserted bits of industry phraseology. "Police and sheriff's deputies, security guards in their riot gear. They will have clubs, which they like to call batons. Water hoses, mace and everything. Even dogs."

"They will?"

"They always have."

"I'll try to make it."

"If you are a little late, we'll wait."

"Figured you would," and the man hung up.

Pamela cook turned from the window and walked to the elevator which took her to the main floor and Western's baggage carousel where she was to turn over the keys to the two men from Department E.

For the past six months, Cook had been assigned to the Palo Verde Nuclear Generating Power Plant under construction in the White Tanks desert. Before that, her assignment was Skagit I and II, in Washington. With her surreptitous prodding the good people of Sagit County had voted against the nuclear plant and the project was brought to a halt. The Atomic Industrial Forum reported that in the past five years a total of sixty-six nuclear plants had either been cancelled or construction had been halted.

With her work finished in Sagit, and eager for a new assignment, Pamela Cook sent a telegram to Hendricks. "HAVE BULLHORN WILL TRAVEL." Her assignment to Phoenix was to encourage anti-nuclear demonstrations and to write propaganda material, and as often as possible, call in on local radio talk shows. Today was the first time she had been instructed to assist any Department E people.

Pamela easily recognized the two men walking toward her from the description givn her by the office. As they neared the baggage carousel she reached into her shoulder tote bag and brought out a double set of car keys, two business size envelopes and a map of Phoenix.

"Mr. Johnson? Mr. Faber?" Pamela asked with a questioning smile.

Johnson offered his hand, but with the palm up. Pamela realized he was accepting the key, not offering to shake hands.

"I have everything the office ordered. The keys to the '83 Datsun. I'll show you where it is parked. This envelope contains your instructions for the return of the material to the office and a map of Phoenix with the route to and from the Mountain Shadows Hotel to Interstate 10 and into Los Angeles." Pamela handed all the papers to Johnson who as yet had not said a word. "Your parking ticket is on the dash. You will pay on your way out at the gate. It will be ninety cents."

Johnson put the envelope and map in his inside coat pocket and handed one set of keys to Faber.

Pamela waited uncomfortably for some response and receiving none said, "This way gentlemen." She led the way to the parking garage and pointed to the black Datsun.

Faber was putting the key in the door when Johnson asked, "Can we drop you someplace or do you have a car?"

"One of my people will pick me up in front of the terminal in a few minutes, but thanks anyway," then Pamela took a white file card from her bag and offered it to Johnson. "This is my office number, address and a map showing how to find it, just in case."

Johnson snapped the card from her hand and got into the car. Pamela watched them back out and start down the winding ramp. "Who the fuck do Department E people think they are?" she said as the Datsun made for the exit. She turned and with long strides started up the auto ramp.

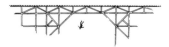

"Only a few blocks more," Burt said as they drove west on Camelback Road. "It should be on the left."

The briefcase was on the front seat between Mary and Burt. Leaving the hotel they had driven west on Lincoln Drive, then south on 24th Street to Camelback Road where they headed west again. Burt was looking for 1621 East Camelback.

While Mary was dressing, Burt had gone through the Yellow Pages trying to locate the nearest Mini-Storage warehouse. He read the half page advertisement aloud, "U Lock It You Keep The Key... 1621 East Camelback Road." That was the closest.

"I wish we had eaten breakfast," Mary complained as she noted the street numbers. "I'm hungry, I'm tired and I'm scared. I've never done anything like this before."

"Neither have I for God's sake," snapped Burt. "This isn't at all like me. It's a damn dream."

"It's a damn nightmare."

"I have never wanted money. Not big money. My income satisfies my needs." Burt was attempting to explain his dilemma to Mary and perhaps at the same time find a clinical rationale for his unaccustomed behavior. "I have many very wealthy patients, and most of them I really don't like," Burt said pointedly. "I have a neighbor, George Foster, worth millions. He's not too bad. But his wife. After his first wife died he met a waitress in New York, and in a week he married her. A perfect parvenu. Everytime she comes over to the house she is dripping with diamonds, and she insists on telling you how much each is worth. Not just the first time, but every time she comes over. A real bore."

Mary kept looking out the side window, hardly listening as Burt went on.

"One night I had this awful dream. This wasn't my usual bad dream. In this dream I was in their new Mercedes, and they were taking me someplace. Mrs. Foster was driving and I was alone in the back seat. For some reason I asked what time it was, and she said, 'I see by my twenty-thousand dollar diamond studded watch it is...'". At that moment we are on a railroad track and a fast freight strikes us broadside. The car is torn to bits. Flying apart, but like in slow motion. The windshield crashes out and cuts off Mrs. Foster's arm. As it goes spinning through the air like a bloody baton, she looks up and sees her arm and she screams, "MY GOD. MY RINGS."

"A combination lock would be better." Mary said flatly.

"Combination lock? I was telling you about the dream I had about my rich-bitch neighbor. What combination lock?"

"The ad you read said, You keep the Key."

"So?"

"You can't telephone a key."

"What the hell are you talking about?"

"I think if you do this whole thing on the telephone it would be a lot safer. You can telephone a combination. I'm only trying to help." Mary pointed toward a large yellow sign. "There it is. Mini Storage."

Burt drove the Lincoln into the driveway of the storage complex. Five long, narrow concrete block buildings with garage type steel doors every twenty feet and no windows. Burt stopped at the door marked OFFICE.

Turning to Mary, Burt said, "You stay in the car and keep the doors locked." He went into the office. On the counter was an old fashion page bell with a sign drawn in blue crayon. 'RING BELL FOR SERVICE.' Burt tapped the bell and waited. When he tapped the bell a second time a door opened at the rear of the narrow office. The elderly man who came through the door seemed to be wearing the popular 'fun-shop' gag. A large pink papermache nose, heavy dark rim glasses and massive bushy black eyebrows flairing above the glasses. When the man came closer Burt saw it was not a gag. The old man indeed had a a large pink nose, wore dark rimmed glasses and his bushy black eyebrows flared from his glasses.

"Yes, sir. Can I help you?" asked the manager.

"I need a small storage unit."

"For how long?"

Before Burt could answer the man was saying, "What you gonna store? We don't allow no guns, or ammunition, or gasoline and stuff like that."

"Just a few boxes," Burt explained.

"Boxes?"

"Some file boxes. I'm moving to Phoenix. Looking for an office."

"You want to rent by the week or by the month?"

Burt was tempted to ask if they rented by the hour, but he said, "A week should be long enough."

"That will be eighteen dollars and fifty cents plus tax. That will be cash or check. Do you need a lock?"

"Yes, I do. A heavy...combination lock, if you have one?"

"We got lots of 'em." The man brought a cardboard box from under the counter. "This is a good one. The combination is in this sealed envelope. Three dollars and fifty cents and we don't take none back. Company policy."

The manager placed a large diagram of the buildings on the counter and with a blue crayon he indicated which space he had allotted to Burt. "This one right here. Number 207. Down the last alley. Got big numbers on the doors. Can't miss it. What name do I put down?"

A name? Burt Cummins couldn't give his name. There on the counter, in a dirty glass ashtray, was a crumpled empty cigarette package with blue printing. "Vantage," Burt replied as he handed the man behind the counter a twenty and a five. Then smiling, said, "Maybe you have heard of our jingle, 'Take Advantage of Vantage'."

"Sounds corny, but it's your company."

Burt took his change and the lock and went back to the car. When Mary saw him she reached over and unlocked the door. "We have space 207. Down the last alley behind the building." Burt said as he started the engine.

"Are you going to get a lock?" Mary asked.

"I got one. A combination lock," Burt said pointedly.

"You bought it here?"

"Why not. The combination is sealed in an envelope."

"Who sealed it?"

Burt pulled out on Camelback Road again. "Watch for a hardware store."

After a short drive, Burt found a True Value and bought another combintion lock and then headed back to the mini-storage and stall 207. When he raised the steel door the inside seemed as large as a livingroom. He thought of the single briefcase sitting alone, completely out of proportion, but, he told himself, it was the value and the safety, not the size that mattered. Burt placed the briefcase in the far corner of the stall, pulled the heavy door down and locked it and spun the combination wheel. He gave a few tugs on the lock and walked back to the car.

"You sure you put the new one on?"

"Yes, I'm sure. The old one is under the seat."

"Can we go eat now? I'm about ready to faint."

The place Burt finally found was a psuedo French cafeteria with inside-sidewalk cafe-style seating. Green and white umbrellas over each table that carried advertisements for Kanterbali, Cini Tonic and Recard. French cuisine menu, French wine in small carafes next to the coffee urn. Backgrund music was a musett tone accordion playing 'The Last Time I Saw Paris' and 'La Vien Rose.' Most important for the choice of this restaurant was not the menu but rather the large windows that made up the walls facing Camelback Road and 24th Street. From the table he picked in the corner Burt felt he could spot any danger that might confront him. The fact that what or who might represent that danger was completely unknown didn't seem to matter. He only knew someone from somewhere at sometime would approach him and he wanted to be ready. Or, at least, feel he was ready.

Mary was eating her Quiche Lorraine in silence. Burt was taking small bites of sweet pastry and large swallows of coffee.

Looking over Mary's shoulder into the busy intersection, Burt began almost to himself. "Greed is a disease of the mind. A form of insanity. One would think I'd have built up some resistance, be immune to the virus. I have certainly been exposed." Waving a bit of pastry to accent a point, "It is a disease you know. Professor Cannon at Harvard proved that. He explained that greed, in a way, is very much like the common cold. You always carry the sickness lying dormant in your psyche. Then, when you are in a weakened condition, POW."

Mary looked up from her plate. "Pow?"

"If I were treating a patient for the condition I am going through, my diagnosis would be 'obsessive neurosis,' but to paraphrase Honest Abe, 'He who has himself for a psychiatrist, has a fool for a shrink'."

Mary was holding her coffee cup with the palms of both hands, as if to warm them. "Aren't you being a little rough on yourself? All this worry over greed." Mary put her cup down. "Greed is when you want to take from others. Take what others need. What is rightfully theirs. If you were taking food from those who were hungry, when you already had plenty to eat, that would be greed."

"I still feel guilty, and frightened."

"Conscience makes cowards of us all," Mary recited with a sigh.

Mary's voice struck Burt like a dart from ambush. "What is that supposed to mean?" he demanded."

"I don't know," Mary said simply. "It's just a quotation of the Bard I remembered from high school lit class. A teacher of mine once tried to explain the writing of Shakespear. He said we fear most what we understand the least. We don't know who these people are or what they might do. It seemed to fit the occasion."

"I don't get the connection."

"All I was trying to say was that what you are doing has nothing to do with greed. Not what I call greed."

"To be willing to risk your life for money, money you don't need... that's plain greed."

"It's plain stupid."

"I admit it's stupid, but I didn't ask for any of this. I wanted only to have a nice, sort of vacation, give my little talk and... Oh my God. My talk. I haven't even looked at the pages of the speech. What time is it?"

"You have the watch."

Burt checked his wristwatch. "Three o'clock. The meeting is at seven."

"You should try to get some sleep," Mary suggested.

"How could I sleep? They are probably waiting for me at the hotel."

"So you tell them if they want their dope back...Let's Make A Deal," Mary said with full gestures.

"It's not funny and keep your voice down." Burt looked around to see if anyone was watching them. "We'll go back to the hotel. You can wait for me out by the pool, across from our room. After they make contact with me I'll tell them what I want, and when they agree, I'll give it to them."

"As simple as that."

"No one will bother you with all those policemen floating around the place."

"I'll be out there until your meeting is over and that could be hours. I'll be hungry again by then." said Mary.

"Call room service and have them bring whatever you want to your poolside table and sign the check. I'll come to you as soon as I can."

"All right, but I'm scared," Mary protested.

"So am I," said Burt.

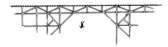

The black Datsun was doing no more than twenty miles an hour when Faber turned into the driveway of the Mountain Shadows Hotel.

Suddenly he slammed on the brakes, locking all four wheels and throwing Johnson's head into the sun visor and his knees into the dashboard.

"What the hell are you doing?" Johnson yelled as he bounced back into his seat.

"Look," Faber said excitedly pointing to the line of police cars in the parking lot.

"So there are police cars. So what?"

"Look how damn many there are."

"They're not after us," Johnson barked. "Now get this toy out of here."

Faber drove slowly past the row of cars. "Do you think they found the stuff?" asked Faber. "Maybe that's why they are here."

"How the hell should I know. Keep driving. Around the hotel. Try to spot that Lincoln."

"Don't get your shit in an uproar with me. It was your idea to put the stuff in his wheel." Faber argued.

"I didn't know you were going to crash into that damn taco wagon and fuckup the whole deal."

As the Datsun headed into the labyrinth of driveways and parking areas that webbed the rear of the hotel, Cummins pulled up to the front entrance and parked in the shade of the canopy.

"Remember," Cummins was telling Mary. "Go to the room and change as quickly as possible. Then go to the pool. You will be safe there. Lots of people always by the pool. Go to the far side and wait for me."

"What if someone sees me? One of them."

"It's my picture they have, not yours."

"What are you going to do now?"

"I'll drop the car at the garage, leave it there. My suit and papers are in the trunk so I'll take a taxi back to the hotel."

"But Burt..."

"When I finish my talk I'll come and get you and we will get out of here. Go somewhere else to stay, so don't worry."

"Sure, don't worry."

"They won't try any rough stuff. Not till they get what they are after," Burt explained. "By then we'll be gone."

Mary leaned over and gave Burt a warm kiss.

"You have the key?" Burt asked.

For an answer Mary dangled the hotel key between her thumb and forefinger and moved out of the car.

Johnson had checked every parking space around the hotel grounds, even a tour of the golf course parking lot and spaces around the tennis courts. Still no white Lincoln with California plates.

On leaving the EMPLOYEE PARKING lot, Johnson said, "Pull back to the front entrance. I'll find out what room Cummins is in."

When the Datsun came to a stop under the awning at the hotel entrance Johnson stepped out and went into the lobby. Several uniformed police were still standing about talking and laughing. Johnson stopped a passing bellman.

"Where are the house phones?" he asked.

"Behind that rock wall, next to the men's room." the man answered pointing directly across the lobby.

"Thanks," Johnson said and made his way through the small groups of talking policemen. When he picked up the house phone a loud buzz could be heard, then a friendly voice said:

"Operator. May I help you?"

"Connect me with Dr. Burton Cummins' room, please."

"One moment," the operator sang.

Johnson could hear the connection being made and the phone ringing.

Mary was standing naked in the center of the room about to step into her new red string bikini when the phone on the little round table began to ring. She stood motionless clutching the handkerchief size material of the bikini and her eyes held on the phone. It couldn't be Burt calling she reasoned. Not in that little time. It could be Mrs. Cummins. The ringing of the phone seemed to be getting louder and more demanding. "It's them," Mary's lips silently mouthed the words. They were calling. Mary forced herself to move and she threw the bikini on the bed next to her purse and took the wrap-around dress from the back of the chair and quickly put it on. The phone kept ringing and it had passed the seven rings the phone company usually suggests. Mary slipped her feet into her shoes and started out the door. When her hand touched the knob she stopped and backed from the door in fear of what might be waiting outside in the parking lot. She turned, her fright building, she grabbed her purse and bikini as she moved past the bed. With one strong pull she slid the glass patio door open and ran down the steps to the pool.

When she reached the bottom step she could still hear the ringing of the phone.

Johnson had been listening to the buzzing of the phone for some time when the operator came back on the line.

"I'm sorry, sir, that room does not answer."

"Are you sure you have the right room?" Johnson asked.

"Yes, sir. Room 212. That is Dr. Cummins room."

"Thank you operator, thank you very much."

Walking rapidly among the sun bathers, past the elegant poolside apartments, Mary found an empty table on the far side in the shade of three tall palm trees. She had hardly moved into the white canvas director's chair when a waiter was at her side with a round serving tray filled with empty plastic glasses.

"May I get something for you from the bar?" he asked.

"Yes, please," Mary gulped a breath of air. "I'll have a large vodka martini."

As the waiter moved away Mary looked across the pool through the splashing water of a dozen swimmers and divers. The patio of room 212 was in clear view. She could see no one near the room. She looked at the inviting water of the pool. And there she sat. Her bikini in her purse and not a stitch under the paisley wrap-around dress. After her martini she would change in the ladies dressing room by the pool, and if no one came out of the patio doors of room 212... she would go for a swim.

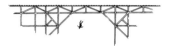

At the Jack Ross Lincoln-Mercury showroom in Scottsdale, only one other man sat in the well appointed customer lounge. In keeping with the theme of the 'West's Most Western Town,' the walls of the lounge were covered with western murals in shades of brown and desert tan. Each wall was a scene depicting ranchlife of years gone by. One scene was a massive roundup with cowboys driving hundreds of longhorn steers down a dusty arroyo. The wall to Cummins' right featured a scene at branding time with a wild eyed calf held down by two cowboys while a third moved toward the animal with a red hot branding iron.

A color television set hung from the ceiling in a far corner of the room. A game show was on, but mercifully the sound was off. In its place melliflous Muzak came from the speakers.

While Cummins waited for transportation to the hotel he studied an elderly man seated across the room from him on a low leather couch. On the wall behind the man was a chuckwagon scene, cowboys lined up with tin plates and cups in their hands, while an assistant cook struck a giant iron triangle hung from the tailgate of the chuckwagon. From the background three more cowboys were at full gallop heading for the noon meal.

The man across the room, who appeared to be in his late seventies, was flipping through magazine after magazine and finally settled for Golf World.

The man wore a tan sport shirt, deep brown casual slacks, highly polished western ankle boots, the typical Sun Belt retiree. Cummins surmised he had migrated to Arizona, living on his savings and monthly check from Social Security. The species is not usually seen this far east of Sun City.

Later, when their eyes met, the old man gave a warm smile, scratched his bald head, then returned his attention to the golf magazine.

Suddenly the man looked up from his reading and apologetically said, "I'm very sorry. I seem to have corralled all the magazines."

He quickly stacked the pile of magazines and negotiated the space between them with movement that belied his apparent age.

"Thanks," said Cummins as he took the magazines and placed them on the couch beside him.

The man turned and went back to his seat and picked up his magazine. "What usually happens," he said, "is when I finally find something of interest to read, they tell me my car is ready."

"You still play?" Burt had wanted the question to sound like, 'You still play, of course,' but it sounded like, 'You still play? At your age?' Burt wished he had remained silent.

"As much as I can," the old man was answering, "A round in the morning, but only nine holes in the evening. I try to dodge the heat."

The elevator-music was interrupted by the voice of the telephone operator.

Mr. Walters, Mr. Art Walters. Your car is ready now. You may pick up your keys at the cashier's window."

"What did I tell you?" The old man said, slapping his magazine down loudly on the seat cushion. "Same thing happens at the barber shop." Then he scratched his bald head and his eyes rolled up as if he were looking at the few remaining hairs. "That is, when I still went to barber shops."

A tall, good looking man hurried into the lounge. His straight black hair, just starting to gray, a thin mustache and a true salesman smile. A man who might harbor political ambitions, but too outgoing and truthful to ever be elected.

As he walked past Cummins he gave him the, "I'll be with you in a moment," nod, then extended his hand to the old man.

"Mr. Walters. I didn't know you were here till I heard the page." He then turned to Cummins.

"Hi. I'm Jack Ross. I run this little store." He gave Cummins a strong handshake. "Mr. Cummins, we are still servicing your car and I have sent a man across town for your hubcap. He hasn't returned yet, so I'll drop you off at your hotel and we'll bring your car around when it's ready, if that is alright with you."

"That will be just fine," said Cummins.

"Have you two met? Mr. Cummins this is Art Walters."

They shook hands.

"Let me help you to the car with your things." Ross said to Cummins as he took his garment bag to the waiting car.

After the good-byes to Mr. Walters, Jack Ross drove his new Lincoln, with dealer plates, up Scottsdale Road and turned west on Lincoln Drive.

"I like to tell visitors that they named this road Lincoln Drive because so many of my customers live along here." Ross said lightly.

"This town has sure grown in the few years I have been away."

"Did you live in the Valley?"

"No. Just over on business from time to time."

"What type business is that?"

"I'm a doctor. Psychiatry."

"You're on vacation?"

"Seminar."

"Interesting. What branch of psychiatry? I ask like I know psychiatry has branches." Ross laughed at himself.

"There are many. I have a general practice on the coast, but I am doing some special research on human reaction under stress. Reaction to sudden and emotional events in peoples' lives. Their reaction to strong stimulus...for good or bad."

"Like?"

"Take for example that old man, Mr. Walters. If he should wake up tomorrow and find he had two million dollars. What do you think his reaction would be?"

"Probably have a massive heart attack. He has five million now."

Cummins rode silently for the remainder of the drive.

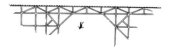

The Datsun was winding its way through the back driveways and parking areas of the Mountain Shadows Hotel. Past the date palms, tall saguaros and short barrel cactus, the flaming bougainvilla, set out in concrete rimmed islands.

"There it is. Room 212." Johnson was pointing from inside the Datsun. "Park over there where I have a clear view of the door."

Faber drove the car in a tight circle around an island of cactus and backed into an empty parking space that gave them an unobstructed view of the door to room 212.

"I'll wait here in the car. You go around and watch the front," Johnson ordered.

"What if he's already found the stuff? What do we do then?" asked Faber.

"That Lincoln pulls in, we'll know soon enough what to do."

"What should I do if I see the guy?"

"Nothing. I want to check out that wheel first, then if we have to, we go after him."

"What about her?" Faber asked pointedly.

"Her?" snapped Johnson.

"That good-lookin' broad he has with him. What we gonna' do with her?"

"Get this through that fat skull. We do nothing with her. You do nothing with her. We get what we came after and we get out of here as fast as we can and as quiet as we can. Now get off your dead ass and keep your eyes open."

Faber had a strong impulse to argue, but thought better of it and let his answer be the loud slamming of the Datsun door.

Burt Cummins walked quickly through the lobby of the hotel carrying his garment bag high on his left shoulder attempting to hide at least half of his face.

Jack Ross had left him off at the hotel entrance after promising his car would be delivered as soon as it was ready. The keys would be under the floor mat on the driver's side. Cummins had arranged payment for these contingencies by leaving his Master Charge number and signature with the cashier.

"Enjoy your stay doctor. When you are back in the valley don't hesitate to call if we can be of service." Ross then drove away.

The Maitre'd was coming on duty and was standing by the red velvet rope which barred the entrance to the still empty dining room. He was wearing a white dress shirt with large silver cufflinks, but had not yet put on his black tuxedo jacket, which he now carried over his arm. As he marked off his reservation list, Cummins interrupted.

"Excuse me. Is there a dressing room where I could change?"

The maitre'd looked up from his chart. "Dressing room?"

"Near the Papago Room, if possible," Burt studied the man's puzzled expression. "I'm speaking this evening in the Papago Room. Is there some place where I could change clothes?"

"We have a band room," the maitre'd offered. "It's not much of a dressing room, but you are welcome to use it, sir." He then unsnapped the brass coupling on the velvet rope to allow Cummins through.

Cummins followed the man as he wound his way among the empty tables and the scurrying waitresses who were setting out silver and tall amber drinking glasses. Busboys were placing a single red rose in each crystal bud vase. Cummins was led across the polished dance floor and through swinging doors into the kitchen. The mingled aromas of baking ham, standing rib roast, turkey and broiled fish filled the steamy air. Teams of cooks in their white ill-fitting blouses, neckerchiefs and chefs' hats that looked like giant white mushrooms atop their heads, watched anxiously while the chief chef sniffed from pot to pot.

Leaving the kitchen Cummins and the maite'd went down a long service hallway.

"The main banquet room is on the other side of this wall," the man said waving his hand to the left. "It runs the full length of the building. We can seat more than seven hundred. Or we divide it into smaller rooms by means of sliding wall sections that hang on overhead tracks. Tonight we will be using only two."

"Which is the Papago Room?" Cummins asked.

"The last one on the left."

The man opened a large door at the end of the hallway, stepped inside the room and switched on an overhead light.

"This is it," the maitre'd said with an apologetic tone as he moved to one side to allow Cummins to enter. "You have chairs, a dressing mirror, a card table and you'll find the toilet behind that far door. Like I said, it isn't much, just a place for the musicians to leave their instrument cases while they are on the stand."

"It will do fine. Thank you." Cummins surveyed the room. "I have a short talk to study and then change into my suit."

"The hotel should have arranged a room for you, sir."

"I have a room," Cummins quickly explained. "My wife is sleeping, not feeling well, I didn't want to disturb her."

"We won't be serving till six-thirty," looking at his watch, "it is five now, may I send back some coffee, or would you care for anything more?"

"Coffee would be plenty, thank you."

The maitre'd left Cummins alone in the room that was not only a band room, but doubled as storage for broken lamps, folding tables with bent legs, throw rugs and many empty cardboard boxes. Still it was as good a place as any to wait. It was a better place than most to hide. Cummins readily admitted he was hiding.

Once again the fear was slowly building as he imagined those coming for the three plastic bags were already at the hotel, walking the grounds, looking for him.

This reaction was by now expected, though far from being controlled. It was a condition apart from himself now. He could hold this fear up in his hands, turn it slowly and examine it from all sides. Study it and appraise it as he would an object of art. But it could never be put in a special place. Locked away. Hidden from others and not from himself. God knows he tried. Hours of excogitation had been spent going back through the years. Back to his childhood. Back to the first time anyone yelled "SCAREDY-CAT."

Burt Cummins was no more than nine years old. All of the neighborhood kids would walk along the railroad tracks north of the little Michigan town to the trestle that crossed a deep, rock-filled ravine. The popular game, similar to follow-the-leader, was to climb out on the steel girders under the trestle and hang from the lowest cross-beam while a mile long freight train roared overhead. Kids in Ravenna had been doing this for years and none had ever been injured. Young Cummins envisioned what could happen if the vibration set up by the train was so great it would shake you off, or if a live coal fell from the engine's fire-box and struck you and burned you so bad that you lost your grip. If someone did fall to the bottom of the ravine he would surely have been killed. Burt did not think the kids were brave who played this game. He was sure they were stupid and he said so.

"SCAREDY-CAT, SCAREDY-CAT," they chanted.

"I'm not a scaredy-cat," he defended himself. "I think this is a dumb thing to do." Then he turned and walked the mile back to his home and he could hear the taunting of the kids and carried that tag, now almost a nickname, through most of his school years. Like Jack the Ripper, Attila the Hun, it was Cummins the Scaredy-Cat.

During the summer vacation of the following year, when no classmates were around, young Cummins walked alone to the trestle. He stood back and studied the narrow beams the other kids had walked on and crawled over and hung from. He remembered the overpowering roar of the speeding train as it sped over the bridge. And he could hear the jeers directed at him... "Cummins is a coward, Cummins is a coward..." taunting him with their sing-song chant.

The intention of this solitary walk to the trestle that day was for him to climb out to the very center, the highest point from the ground, and hang from the lowest beam and wait for the afternoon train. This would prove he was no 'scaredy-cat.' But, the longer he viewed the structure and the threatening boulders a hundred feet below, the more his resolution diminished. If he did climb out under the trestle and if he did hang there until the freight went over, who would believe him? So why risk it? Cummins walked back to town along the railroad track, throwing stones at the glass insulators on the telegraph poles along the right of way.

That night, as he lay in his bed, he heard the shrill whistle of the midnight express giving its warning to the county road crossing. The train was heading north, across the flat land and the Crockery Creek trestle. Cummins could hear the driver wheels pounding on the steel rails, the rhythm pattern of clanks as the freight's wheels went over the rail joints, the change in tone when the engine was on the trestle.

"I should be under there right now," he was challenging himself. "I would show them. No one ever dared do it at night, in the dark. Not one of them. Tomorrow night I'm going to do it. I'll show them who is a 'scaredy-cat'..."

Later, in his sleep, a disjointed playful dream suddenly became horrific. He was on the trestle. There was shouting and laughter. Hands were forcing him on to the narrow steel beam. A girl's voice rang out, "Hurry, the train's coming. Hurry." Then another, "Get out on that beam, scaredy-cat." He was now hanging over the lowest beam. The I beam cutting his waist. Far below he could see the rocks at the bottom of the ravine. Then there were crowds of people on the concrete trestle supports. All yelling and shouting. A hand reached out and lifted his feet over his head. He was slipping head first. He tried to reach the beam but his hands were too small. He was holding with his fingers and they were not strong enough to bear his weight. He was swinging his legs and kicking in a desperate attempt to regain the beam. The noise of the steam engine crowded out the yelling of the kids and the crowd. The steel members of the trestle were shaking and the vibration was building. Then a violent shudder of the beam ripped itself loose from his grasp and he began to fall. His underview of the trestle moving away from him and as his body rotated the jagged rocks and boulders were rushing at him...A jolt, a sting, and nine year old Burton Cummins was awake. His face was wet with sweat. His body trembling. This was not the first time such a dream had ripped his night and it was not to be the last.

Cummins hung his garment bag on the clothes rack, already cluttered with wire hangers. He unzipped the bag's side and reached in to retrieve the loose typewritten pages Professor Hamilton had prepared for his speech. Moving to the round card table he set the pages on the green felt cover, rimmed with cigarette burns. He began shuffling the papers into proper sequence. The air conditioning hadn't caught up with the heat of the room and Cummins removed his coat and placed it over the back of a bentwood chair. While sorting the pages, a waiter brought a tray with silver coffee pot and matching cream and sugar server, a large cup and a bright red napkin wrapped around a heavily tooled spoon.

"Will that be all, sir?" asked the waiter, while placing the tray on the table, being careful not to disturb the pages.

Cummins gave two one dollar bills to the waiter, "Thank you, very much."

When the waiter had gone, Cummins looked at his open wallet. Sticking up from the credit card section was the business card of the U LOCK MINI STORAGE CO. On the reverse side of the card he had written the numbers of the combination lock that now hung on the storage room door. L 12-2, R 99-2, L 24-2. Cummins looked at the card for a long moment. He could see the briefcase in the corner of the storage unit. The three green plastic bags inside... Where would it end? When would it end?

His breathing became heavy as a parade of fears filed through his mind. His wife at home. They wouldn't have reason to harm her. If he would ask her to move to a hotel for a few nights, it would worry her. Might be too much for her heart. And Mary, it's going to be a longer wait for her than he thought it would. Perhaps he should go to her now. Have her wait in the band room till he finished his talk. He couldn't go walking around the hotel. They must be here by now. Would they try to call him? Would he be able to hear the page from the lobby if they did call? They won't do anything until they have made contact with him. This he was sure of.

Cummins poured his coffee with a steady hand and began reading the pages from Professor Hamilton.

"Ladies and gentlemen. It gives me a great deal of pleasure to address such a distinguished gathering and to speak to a most important subject. A subject we in the profession must investigate to the fullest for the protection of, not only our patients, but the citizens of our nation..."

By six-thirty that evening, most of the guests around the pool had retreated to their rooms to dress for the evening meetings or for supper and dancing.

Mary Parker had long ago finished her first double vodka martini and changed to her red string bikini in the ladies dressing room at poolside.

For the first hour she lay full length on a bright yellow plastic lounge chair. The terror brought on by the ringing telephone had not fully subsided, but an hour of warm sunshine had lessened her tension sufficiently for her to enjoy the exiguous thrill of an appreciative male glance or low wolf whistle directed her way. She giggled inwardly when the older men walking by would attempt to draw in their bulging stomachs, thinking she was evaluating them from behind her dark sun glasses.

After her second vodka martini and club sandwich, with all the trimmings, Mary waited the mandatory thirty minutes before slipping into the luxuriousness of the pool.

When the sun went down behind Squaw Peak the sky became slate gray and underwater lights illuminated the bottom of the pool. Powerful floodlights, placed around the base of the tall palm trees threw a golden glow on the gently waving green fronds high overhead.

Mary was gliding through the water with strong, smooth strokes when she heard the voice of the hotel security guard.

"Sorry people, the pool is closed."

"Closed?" Mary questioned in disappointment.

"We have to vacuum the pool and the aerator will be turned on in a few minutes."

Mary made one more leisurely lap of the pool and was the last to climb the steps at the shallow end.

With the loss of the sun the air quickly cooled several degrees and Mary was struck with a sudden chill. She took her wrap-around dress from the chair, picked up her shoes and purse and padded barefoot across the wet, slippery cement to the ladies dressing room and found the door locked. A small sign on the door read, 'OPEN 9 AM to 6 PM.' The sign could not be seen when the door was open as it had been during the day.

Mary was now shaking visibly. Partly from the cold and partly from disgust. To herself she reasoned, I can't use the ladies room in the hotel lobby...not dressed or undressed like this, then aloud she said, "SHIT."

Hearing the sound of gushing water Mary looked back to see the aerators had been turned on and a high dense spray covered the entire pool, forming a mountain of mist. The underwater lights gave substance to the mountain, like a golden effervescent champagne-cloud floating on the surface of the pool.

Mary could no longer stand there. Her shaking had become uncontrollable. She knew where there was a towel, lots of towels. Dry clothes, everything she needed. Room 212. She would only be in the room a few minutes. If the phone rang again she would let it ring.

Quickly, around the foaming pool, through the empty tables and chairs and up the stone steps to the patio of room 212. Mary saw the drapes were fully drawn across the entrance, but the sliding glass door was partly open. She could not remember if she had closed it when she ran out of the room. Probably not. There was no one around, that she could see, and by now she was nearly freezing. Into the room, Mary slid the door closed behind her and went directly to the bathroom and turned on the heatlamps in the ceiling. She untied the two small bows at her hips and let the wet bikini fall to the tile floor. Taking a large bath towel from the wall rack she began to dry herself. She rubbed her arms and stomach, patted and blotted her breasts and shoulders. Placing her left foot on the edge of the tub she bent from the waist to rub her leg dry. Droplets of water fell from her hair and she made a quick decision to wrap her head in a towel and dry her hair later when she was dressed and back by the pool.

At the moment Mary brought her left foot to the floor, a faint wisp of air felt cool on her damp skin. She raised her right foot to the edge of the tub and bent again to dry herself when she was startled by the sudden pressure of two strong arms thrown tightly around her naked waist. The coarse material of a coatsleeve tore abrasively at her stomach, rough buttons dug at her back. She began to struggle and scream. Mary held the towel tightly and fought to fend off her attacker with swinging elbows. The man's powerful arms were lifting her from the floor. She screamed again. As she was being dragged and carried backwards from the bathroom she made a desperate grab for the towel rack. Mary's fingers had barely touched the rack when a vicious tug at her midsection took her out the door with her feet kicking clear of the floor. She was lifted sideways into the air and carried into the room and thrown down crossways of the bed, with the full weight of the fat man on her like a wrestler forcing an opponent to the mat. Mary was still trying to free herself. Her face was twisted in fright. Holding the towel in front of her for what little protection it might give, she kicked and squirmed and tossed from side to side, but was not able to free herself from the man who was now forcing her back by gripping each of her wrists and holding them above her head.

"Where's your boyfriend, honey?" the fat man asked as he pressed all his weight against her arms.

From somewhere, Mary found the breath to yell at the fat man. "Get away from me."

With both arms held above her head, the towel had fallen to her side. Her attacker, breathing in gasps, took a moment to let his eyes move over her nude body.

"I don't want to hurt you none, honey," he grunted with sweat running down his face. "We just want your boyfriend, the doctor." He shook her violently, "Where is he?"

"I don't know. I don't know," Mary cried.

Faber was above her now twisting her wrists, sending shocks of pain down to her shoulder.

"I think you do," he growled and released her left wrist just long enough to strike her across the face with his open hand, driving Mary's head to the side. He again caught her flying arm and pressed it back to the bed.

"Your good doctor has something of ours and we want it. We want it now, and if we don't get it..." he struck her again in the face on the red welt forming from the first blow.

Again he captured her arm in a vice grip and held it. For a moment Faber entertained the thought of knocking Mary out with a fist to the jaw and to have her unconscious body to do with as he would. While this idea was generating in his head Mary found new strength and was again thrashing left and right in an attempt to free herself from his grasp.

Faber was now forcing large gulps of air through his open mouth. His strong hands still holding Mary's arms above her head while his right leg was pressing on Mary's left knee. He forced his knee between her legs and was trying to pry them apart. He looked down on her. He had read, somewhere, that many women who tried to fight off an attacker really experienced a sexual thrill. In the midst of their kicking and screaming they would experience a forceful orgasm. The magazine also said women were further aroused by sensual kisses on the neck and breasts. Faber was now looking in Mary's face. His sweat dripping onto her wet, matted hair. He raised his left leg in an attempt to straddle her when Mary gave a hard driving knee into his bulging crotch. In pain he rolled back from her for only a second, but it was enough for Mary to twist to the right and pull her arm free and be kneeling on the floor at the side of the bed. If she could reach the phone, knock it to the floor, scream... Mary was about to gain her feet when Faber's arms grabbed her again and flung her across the room, back against the low dresser. Stumbling, Mary put her hands behind her to keep from falling. The man put a crushing bear hug on her, forcing the air from her lungs. He bent her body back against the top of the dresser. Her left fist beating on his face and shoulders, trying hopelessly to loosen his hold. Her free hand went behind her for support and touched the paper flowers of the banderillas. Her fingers desperately stretching to encircle the two sticks. Did she dare try? On which end of the sticks were the steel barbs?

Faber's left hand was now tight on her throat and his mouth, wet with sweat and spittle, was seeking her full breast. He felt her body relax. His mouth was on her breast, his tongue slobbering circles around the nipple. She was giving herself to him. Faber felt her press her body to him. Her left hand moved slowly up his arm, her long fingernails digging lightly at the short hair at the back of his neck. He was going to have her, "By God, the magazine was right."

Mary moved her left shoulder in a way that left no doubt she was offering her breast to him. He had her now. He adjusted his hold on her so he might better please her with his searching tongue. Mary swung her right hand high above her head. Stopped for a split second at the apex, then drove the two barbs deep into the fat man's spine... perfect placement, right between the shoulderblades.

78

Faber made no sound, only a harsh intake of air. He did not come after her. He released his hold and sank slowly to his knees. Mary moved to the side. The man was on all fours and, with one hand on the edge of the dresser, he pulled himself to his feet, still in a bent-over position. Agony and disbelief on his face. A dribble of blood coming from Faber's mouth. His hands groping desperately to reach the center of his back, but they could not extend to the source of his pain.

Mary backed away another step.

Faber turned, and at a drunken run, swung the drapes back on the patio door with his left hand, his right still trying to reach the sticks which stood out straight from his back.

He stumbled his way down the four stone steps, across the pool deck and disappeared into the golden mist of the aerated water...

Mary watched after the man as he went into the pool. She was crying. Her hair matted and drawn in a series of lines across her flushed face. She put the back of her hand to her left cheek and tried to draw air into her starved lungs. She could still feel the sting from the vicious slap to her face. There was fire around her wrists. She wanted to run. Run anywhere. She yanked the drapes closed to shut out the sight of the pool. "I must find Burt, I must find Burt," she kept repeating through tears.

Mary made her way to the closet and took a blue slack suit from a hanger and with trembling hands, began to dress.

Burt Cummins finished his talk to the gathered doctors and their wives. At the conclusion he was greeted with light, yet polite, applause. Not like the reception his address earned at their last meeting. It was probably his own fault for not giving enough time to review and edit Professor Hamilton's material, and too, his mind was not one hundred percent on the presentation. Some of the findings he read from the pages were, for him, rather radical and perhaps disturbing to a great many in his audience. Now it was over and Cummins was happy for that.

When he returned to the band room three of the seven musicians had arrived and were taking their instruments out of their cases. Without a word Cummins went to the pipe rack and began changing to his sport coat and pullover, short sleeve shirt. He would wear the same pants and shoes, no one would notice at night.

Cummins overheard some small talk among the musicians and jokes, and a question and comment on the jazz festival that had run on

HBO the night before, their only night off. Two more members arrived and there were more greetings. Cummins was by now nearly changed. The tenor man had his horn out and was running scales with the bell of his saxophone inches from the full-length mirror. He kept adjusting the horn's mouthpiece.

The next musician to enter the room was the youngest so far. He had a small black chin beard giving the man a Lincolnesque appearance. This was the drummer and he entered with a flair.

"You guys see all that 'fuzz' around the pool?"

"Some kind of cop's convention," the piano man put in.

"They have more than a convention, they got real on-the-job training. I just saw them taking some guy's body out of the pool. He really took the Lipton Plunge. He was floating face down out there. And get this, sticking out of his back were two of those bullfight sticks. You know, like they stick in the bull. This fat guy was floating out there with those things sticking up like a harpooned whale that was marked for a later pick-up. Real Moby Dick stuff."

Cummins pulled his garment bag from the rack and ran from the room, bumping into the last musician to arrive.

"Who was that masked man?" the drummer asked the room.

"Beats the hell out of me," said the piano man.

The sax man at the mirror was saying, "God damn these plastic reeds."

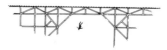

Cummins was almost running along the narrow hallway, dodging waiters balancing trays of food. Through the crowded kitchen and out the swinging door, he crossed the still empty dance floor. The maitre'd made an attempt to say, "Good evening, doctor," but his words trailed off because Cummins was well into the lobby. Small groups had gathered talking in low tones, probably about the man in the pool with the two Mexican banderillas in his back.

"For God's sake, Mary... where are you?" Cummins asked as he went out the double doors leading down the wide steps to the pool.

The scene was like a Beverly Hills 'Come As You Are Party,' held around a movie star's pool. Here the curious were at all levels of the veranda, tending tall drinks in their hands. The men dressed in tuxedos, busines suits and sports wear. The ladies in formals, cocktail dresses and slack-suits. All attention was directed to the five police-men and three plainclothes detectives from homicide who were by the edge of the pool, surrounding the odd form under a plain gray blanket.

The shape of the blanket reminded Cummins of a make-do pup-tent he once had as a kid in his back yard. This pup-tent looked like one end pole had fallen.

Water, with a tinge of pink, was seeping rivulets from under the blanket onto the white pool decking.

Cummins' eyes went anxiously from face to face along the bannis-ter. He surveyed the few who were watching from across the pool.

Two uniformed policemen lifted the blanket off the body and an officer from the photo bureau took flash pictures at various angles.

Some of the onlookers turned away from the grim sight. Others stood on chairs and strained for a better view. One lady was heard to say, "I wish I had my camera."

Cummins began walking among the crowd, circling the scene and trying to locate Mary. He could find her nowhere. It crossed his mind that she might have gone back to their room. His path was blocked by two ambulance attendants pushing a four-wheel stretcher. While he waited for them to pass, a voice spoke to him over his left shoulder.

"That's really somethin', isn't it?"

Cummins turned and was looking into the face of the D.E.A. man. For a moment he couldn't remember his name, but there was no mistaking the red walrus mustache.

"Looks gruesome down there," Burt said, then protectively, "It must have happened while I was giving my talk."

The two ambulance attendants stopped short of the body and stood back and waited for the investigation to continue.

"What's it all about? Do they know who he is?" Cummins asked and wished he hadn't.

"They are still putting it together for the coroner's report. Information is sketchy so far." The redhead took a small notebook from his inside pocket and flipped over a few pages, turned two back down. "Name, Karl Faber. He's not registered at this hotel. California drivers license, expired six years ago so the L.A. address may not be good."

The D.E.A. man closed his notebook and once again looked down at the scene by the pool. "Those Mexican bullfight things in his back," he said finally, "that's what sets this case apart."

"Banderillas," Cummins offered.

"What?"

"Banderillas... that is what they call those bullfight things."

The D.E.A. man opened his notebook again. "How do you spell it?"

"B A N D," (maybe I could have a dentist wire my mouth shut), thought Cummins, "E R I L L A S."

"I've heard the word, but I couldn't remember." The man put the notebook in his pocket.

"You have quite a lot of information already," said Burt. "Are you... that is, the D.E.A., interested in this case?"

"We might be. They found three little McDonald's spoons in his pocket."

"McDonald's spoons?"

"He may just like McDonald's coffee...or he could have used those little spoons to measure heroin. It's being done a lot. We'll have a lab report."

82

"Sounds like Sherlock Holmes."

"Not really...or should I say 'elementary'?" The D.E.A. man laughed lightly. "It is the run-or-the-mill information every man carries in his pockets and his wallet."

Cummins felt that cold sweat breaking out again. He was thinking of the wallet in his back pocket, the Mini-Storage card with the combination to the lock written on the back.

"We once had a man proven guilty of murder because he didn't throw away a street-car transfer. The transfer gave the name of the street, direction of travel, the time of day and the date. The murder took place at the transfer point and the suspect forgot that when you board the next car the conductor takes the transfer. There was much more to it, but sometimes a little mistake like that can start an alibi to unravel and break a case wide open."

A uniformed police officer came up to the D.E.A. man and told him the homicide people wanted to talk with him.

"They want me down there. See you later?"

"Sure."

"Maybe have a drink after this slows down. You are in 212?"

"Right."

The redhead followed the policeman to the pool.

"He knows something," Cummins was talking to himself. "That red haired son-of-a-bitch knows something. Why else would he be telling me all that?"

Cummins started walking up to room 212.

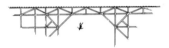

Robert Johnson was awakened by the bright highbeam headlights shining directly on his closed eyes. He squinted against the pain. His eyes opened a slit to the intense glare through the Datsun windshield. Johnson vaguely remembered it had been daylight when he dozed off, and from that doze he had fallen into a deep, though restless, sleep. Now it was dark.

The car, whose headlights had aroused him to wakefulness, swung into the parking space directly ahead of him. It was a white Mark VI. License plate orange on blue. California. It was THE LINCOLN.

The driver turned off the ignition and the headlights. When he opened the car door the interior lights came on and Johnson could see the driver was not the doctor.

Johnson reached down and brought a lug wrench from under the seat. The wrench had a socket on one end and was formed into a wedge on the other.

The driver bent to put the keys and receipt under the floor mat, then got out of the Lincoln and closed the door. He hadn't gone ten yards when Johnson was out of the Datsun and walking lightly to the left front wheel of the Mark VI. Down on one knee he quickly removed the hubcap which he let fall to the ground. It began to cartwheel down the slope of the parking lot. The hubcap rolled only a few feet then fell to its side and spun to a noisy stop like a spinning quarter on a tavern bar.

Hearing the noise the driver turned to see Johnson still on his knee by the front wheel.

"Hey, you." the driver yelled. "What the hell do you think you're doing?"

The driver started running toward the man he saw kneeling by the front wheel. When he was within five feet of Johnson, he yelled again. "Get the hell away from that..." Johnson turned hard, the lug wrench swinging in his hand. He struck the young man across the temple and he fell to the ground like a sledged steer in a slaughter house.

Johnson moved over the fallen man, who now lay face down on the tarmac. He struck three heavy blows to the head of the driver and then threw the lug wrench into the thick oleander bushes that lined the parking lot.

With two easy moves, Johnson rolled the body over and, putting a hand under each arm, he pulled the limp figure into the oval cactus bed. Johnson picked up a large rock from the garden and smashed the blue floodlight that had been placed on the ground to display the many types of cactus at night. Now the body was wedged between two barrel cactus. Their sharp needles drawing blood from a thousand punctures in the man's skin.

Walking back, past the Lincoln, Johnson went up to the door of 212. He knocked firmly on the door with his left hand as his right went to his shoulder holster and the snub nose .38.

Mary was dressed and her crying was now under control. She adjustd a thick towel around her wet hair, giving it the style of an Indian turban. She allowed herself a moment of lightness as she thought that all the towel needed was a precious jewel or flashy bauble pinned on the front.

The knock on the door startled Mary to her shoes. Let it be Burt, was her silent prayer.

She moved to the door and with her ear near the chain-lock she called, "Burt? Is that you?"

"We brought your car back, lady," Johnson said through the door.

"Thank you," Mary answered.

There was a pause, "You have to sign for it," said Johnson.

Mary tucked the ends of hair under the towel and took the chain nightlock out of the slot. She began to turn the knob when the door flung open driving her back against the wall. Johnson was in the room with the muzzle of the .38 hard against her throat. Terror was in Mary's eyes as his thumb pulled the hammer back to the second click.

"Where is it? What did you do with it?" Johnson pressed the gun even harder into her neck. "What did you do with it?"

"I don't have it," Mary's voice was nearly chocked off and she was fighting for air.

"You got into the hubcap. The stuff is gone. Now, where is it? TELL ME." Johnson shoved his gun so hard under Mary's chin that he forced her head back and her eyes went to the ceiling.

"A man came. He took it," Mary managed to get the words out.

"What man?"

"Some man... A fat man... He came and took it."

"Faber? Faber took the stuff?" Johnson lightened the pressure of the gun for a moment as his mind raced. "When? When did he take it?"

"Ten. Ten minutes ago. I don't know. He busted in with a gun and took the stuff. The stuff in the plastic bags." Mary was crying and lying to save her life. "He made Burt go with him. He said if I called the police he would kill Burt."

"Where did they go?" Johnson demanded, his anger growing.

"I don't know. They went out that door," Mary tried to indicate the glass patio door with a slight movement of her head.

"That dirty bastard. That fat no good son-of-a-bitch." Then, as if a sudden decision had been made. "O.K., let's go." He backed away from Mary, but kept the gun to her stomach and pushed her to the open door.

"Where are you taking me?" Mary protested.

Johnson forced her through the door. "I have someone who wants to hear your story. Now move."

With the gun in her side and a vice grip on her elbow, Johnson ushered her to the black Datsun.

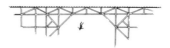

Cummins continued walking to his room and was surprised to find the patio door open. He entered the room, put his garment bag on the back of a chair, and looked around. The bedspread was crumpled. He and Mary could have done that this afternoon. There was a damp bath towel on the floor at the foot of the bed. That figured, too. In the bathroom Burt saw Mary's red bikini on the tile floor, still wet. He picked up the two piece bikini and tossed it into the sink. Cummins went to the closet. Mary's clothes were there and her luggage was on the floor.

"Where is she? Where the hell is she?" he kept saying.

He went out the rear door to the parking area. His Mark VI was in space 212.

"Damn," said Burt, looking at the left front wheel. "They didn't get the hubcap."

The keys were under the floor mat along with the receipt from the garage. Cummins took the keys and receipt and returned to his room. He sat in a chair by the phone. He hadn't slept in two days and nausea was building. He was hungry, but he knew he couldn't eat. He was exhausted and knew he couldn't sleep. His eyes would barely focus as he unfolded the receipt from Jack Ross Lincoln garage. He could make out the bottom line. "ONE 1983 WIRE WHEEL HUBCAP $125.00." Cummins folded the paper. "They charged me for the hubcap but they didn't put it on... Or... did they and someone...?"

The ringing of the phone startled Cummins. His fatigue made the lifting of the receiver a clumsy movement.

"Hello," he said when he finally got the phone to his ear.

"Don't talk. Just listen," a stern voice ordered.

"Doctor Cummins, you are a very fortunate man. You are fortunate because I am a very understanding man. I understand that you were no party to the mechanics of the transporting of my property. You have wisely not gone to the police. Please don't make the fatal mistake of assuming that my understanding is in any way a sign of weakness or indecision. I assure you, it is not..." Hendricks then continued in a very calm voice, "Doctor Cummins, I want my property returned and I want it returned now."

There was a long moment of silence.

"Faber is dead," Cummins said and not knowing why he had said it.

"Faber?"

Hendricks was caught off guard.

"They found him in the pool an hour ago." After a dramatic pause. "It was no accident."

Cummins could hear his own voice, but it was not coming out of his mouth, was it? It was more like talking in a dream. It went on uncontrolled. A recording of your own voice, a recording you could not turn off.

"So?" Hendricks said simply.

"I have your property. It is safe. And I will tell you where it is, for a price."

"And that is?"

"Street value of the three bags is close to two million. I think five hundred thousand would be a fair price."

"Isn't that a little steep?" Hendricks asked. "Your street value estimate, to begin with, is a million high. And my merchandise is not for resale. So, in light of those facts, do you have a more reasonable demand?"

"I think five hundred thousand is a reasonable demand, and one other thing." A part of Cummins' mind was asking 'when are you going to shut up?' still he went on. "You have property that belongs to me. I want Mary Parker returned, unharmed. When she is safe and I have the money, then you will have your property."

"Mary Parker?" Hendricks' voice reflected he had been given an unfamiliar name. "I thought you were asking about your wife."

"My wife?"

"You want to talk to her?"

Cummins slowly stood up holding the phone with both hands. The confidence that had been building was ripped away. In its place was ice. "You have my wife there?"

"Hold on a second and I'll get her for you." Hendricks spoke in a casual, friendly manner, like someone being called to the phone in a friend's house.

Cummins' hands shook as he tried to hold the phone to his ear and he sat down on the edge of the bed.

"Burt?"

"Yes, darling," he recognized his wife's voice at once.

"Who are these people? What do they want?" Mrs. Cummins was crying.

"Are you all right? Have they hurt you?"

"No, not really. What do they want?"

"Please, Martha, try to stay calm. Darling, everything will be cleared up. It's only a misunderstanding."

"Doctor," Hendricks was back on the phone. "Sort of a stand-off, wouldn't you say?"

"Listen, if anything happens to my wife. If you hurt her in any way. Martha has a bad heart and a thing like this could…"

"Doctor, the fate of your wife, and your Mary Parker, is pretty much up to you. Your's too, for that matter."

Cummins was beaten, and he knew it. "What do you want me to do?"

"Stay where you are. We will contact you. And Doctor, keep up the good work. Don't talk to the police. You keep my property safe and I'll do the same for you." CLICK, and Hendricks was gone.

For the next full minute Cummins sat on the bed. His heart pounding. His fear now was for his wife and Mary.

"Oh, God. Please help me."

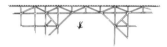

At gunpoint, Johnson forced Mary to drive the Datsun while he relayed directions from the file card Pamela Cook had given him at the airport.

After thirty minutes driving into the downtown section of Phoenix, across the bridges and under freeways, Johnson suddenly motioned Mary to turn left onto a small side street with low industrial type buildings on either side.

As she made the turn, the headlights of the Datsun swept across a sign, LA PALOMA INDUSTRIAL PARK. Several firms were listed, but none were recognizable. Above the building in the night sky, Mary saw the white and green revolving beacon on the control tower at Sky Harbor Airport. She guessed she was a mile south of the runway.

"Stop here," Johnson ordered, flicking his gun toward an open parking space among several 'choppers' and four prime candidates for Rent A Wreck. The car on Mary's left was the pick of the litter. It was a black, '71 Chevy, four KC's on the roof, CB antennas, fore and aft, and trimmed with green marijuana leaf designs on the doors.

"Stay there," Johnson said as he turned off the lights and the engine and took the key. He opened his door by reaching behind him with his right hand. His left hand kept his gun leveled at Mary. Backing out of he car, he closed his door, moved around the front of the Datsun and opened Mary's door.

"Let's go." Johnson had that painful grip on Mary's elbow again and forced her ahead of him, stumbling up to the windowless building and a large wooden door with the numbers '1888' running diagonally from the upper left hand corner.

As Johnson pressed the doorbell he gave an extra hard squeeze to Mary's elbow. "Don't try anything and you won't get hurt."

Mary winced at the sharp pain. "You think a broken arm doesn't hurt?"

"Shut up." Johnson put his gun in his coat pocket.

The door opened to an unexpected blaze of flashing, colored lights, pulsing in rhythm to blasting disco music. A tall man with broad shoulders filled the doorway. A heavy black beard made it tough to judge his age. Long, scraggy hair cascading from under a worn leather cap with greasy Harley-Davidson wings over the bill. The shiny black leather jacket was far newer than the cap, but the rusty chain fourragere on the left shoulder killed any attempt at style.

"Yea?" was his irritable greeting, after which he took a long drink from a tall can of Bud, followed by a noisy belch.

"I came to see Pamela Cook," Johnson was direct.

The man gave an inquisitive look at Johnson and an appraising look at Mary. "She expecting you?"

"Yes. It's important."

"To who?"

"Is she here?"

"Yea."

Johnson pushed Mary into the noise-filled room and the bearded man closed the door behind them. "Wait here," he ordered, then walked into the red and blue haze of the room.

Mary watched the couples gyrating to the disco beat on the concrete area they claimed as a dance floor. The strobe light giving a slow-motion effect to their movements. Other couples were standing, talking and laughing with exaggerated gestures. Some were seated at low, round wooden tables that were once giant cable spools from the local power company.

The unmistakeable essence of marijuana hung over the room like a net. A twenty-year old, Tiffany-faced Wurlitzer jukebox glowed in one corner with its sound coming from hidden speakers in the low ceiling. Next to the jukebox was a coin operated ZIG-ZAG dispenser.

The posters on the walls were difficult to read, but Mary could make out a few. NO NUKES, MAKE LOVE NOT WAR, LEAGALIZE

MARIJUANA, HEAR JANE FONDA AT ARIZONA STATE UNIVERSITY. The others were too far into the dark to read.

Mary's blue knit slack-suit and Johnson's vested Dacron pinstripe were in sharp contrast to the tight jeans and halter tops the girls were wearing. The men wore dirty jeans, boots and cowboy hats crowned with dyed chicken feathers. Their denim jackets had the sleeves cut off to display their multi-tattooed arms.

The bearded man reappeared and motioned with a curled finger to follow him. Before Mary could take a first step, Johnson was shoving her forward causing her to take three quick, short steps to retain her balance but not before she had sent her shoulder into a passing waitress and her tray of drinks.

"I'm sorry," Mary apologized.

The waitress rescued her tray and gave Mary her most exasperated look, then her eyes moved up to the towel wound around Mary's head, and a small smile started that would have become a laugh, if it had the time. The waitress called after Mary, "Can I check your cobra, dear?"

At the back of the room a door was opened and the harsh white light from inside said that if the front room was all play, then this room was all business.

Along one wall of the room Mary saw a wooden picnic table with the words PHOENIX PARKS DEPARTMENT, stenciled across the green top. On the table were stacks of letters, colored brochures, pictures, bumper stickers, boxes of envelopes and a postage meter machine. Five women, dressed much like those in the play room, were seated along one side, busily folding letters and stuffing envelopes. All stopped work, and all eyes were on Mary and Johnson as they entered the room.

Pamela Cook was seated behind a large wooden desk in the corner. She was holding the phone to her ear and with her free hand she waved Johnson to come to her desk, then she turned her full attention back to the phone.

"Damn it to hell," she was yelling, "You dropped the fuckin' ball, that's what you did. You dropped the fuckin' ball."

Pamela cook listened to the person on the other end of the line for a short time with her head wagging from side to side, not at all in agreement with what the other person was saying, and as soon as she could interrupt, she would tell him so.

"I don't buy any of that shit," Cook went on. "You didn't do your job. It's as simple as that.'' Cook picked up a yellow pencil off the top of her desk and threw it down again. "I'll read your report, and so will Hendricks, but it won't do a damn bit of good now.''

Pamela slammed the phone down and shook her head slowly, trying to think of what could be done now to undo the damage one of her operatives caused.

She looked up at Johnson who was standing in front of her desk, still holding Mary's arm.

"That bunch of shitheads in Maine,'' Cook said, still boiling, "They lost the damn election. Those dumb bastards voted to keep their nuclear plants in operation and they will probably build more now. When will people learn the truth? When?''

Pushing her leather chair back, she stood up behind her desk. "I thought you would be on your way to Los Angeles by now,'' her tone expressed her continued disappointment.

"Faber ran off with the shipment,'' Johnson said with the same enthusiasm one might have saying it looks like rain.

"Faber? The fat guy? You're sure?''

"She was there.'' Johnson said, indicating Mary.

"Who the hell is she?''

"The doctor's girlfriend.''

"Girlfriend?'' Pamela snorted. "Looks more like a live-in hooker. I'll bet she could tie a string on a paint roller and use it for a Tampax. Couldn't you deary?''

Mary was about to take up the challenge when Johnson's hold tightened on her arm.

"Where is the doctor?'' Pamela asked, ignoring Mary.

"Faber busted into their room, took the stuff and made the doctor go with him,'' Johnson explained.

"Did Faber take the car?''

"I have the Datsun.''

"They took the doctor's car?''

"No.''

"Maybe they took a taxi,'' Pamela snapped. She was no longer the woman assigned to assist the 'big boys' in Department E. She was the hard, cold interrogator now. Playing this very real role in her own make-believe world. A world where cunning was power.

"Faber can hot-wire any car in thirty seconds. He'll have wheels.'' Johnson offered.

"Good for him.'' Pamla turned and walked behind her chair and leaned over the high back, her long fingers kneading the leather headrest. She had taken the weight of the problem on her shoulders and was putting Johnson on the defensive. Sparring for a position. She knew position would be most important when the office asked questions, and there would be questions, she would see to that.

"Have you notified Mr. Hendricks?" Pamela asked as if it were an unimportant afterthought.

"I wanted to do that from here," Johnson began. "I needed some place to keep her on ice while I made the call."

Pamels leaned over and pushed the phone across the top of the desk toward Johnson. "So call." With a nod toward Mary, "She's not going anyplace."

Mary turned and saw the five women had left their work at the table and were standing threateningly close behind her.

Johnson released Mary's arm for the first time since they entered the building.

"You know the number?" Pamela goated.

"This phone clean?" he asked.

"As a whistle."

Johnson dialed the office number and waited while the phone rang at the other end. Pamela's eyes were on him. Her arms were folded across her chest waiting. She looked from Johnson to Mary and back to Johnson.

When Johnson heard Hendricks' voice, he jumped to attention.

"Hello, this is Johnson. I'm in Phoenix."

"I've been waiting for your call," Hendricks said patiently.

"Things have really gone sour over here, Mr. Hendricks."

"Sour?" Hendricks questioned.

Johnson took a deep breath and changed the phone to his left ear.

"Faber has run off with the shipment, Mr. Hendricks. Took the three bags from that doctor and split. He was supposed to be watching their hotel room for me, but he busted in on them, took the stuff and split."

"He did?" Hendricks said in mock surprise.

"And he took the doctor with him."

"For your information, Johnson, they fished Faber's body out of that hotel swimming pool less than an hour ago."

"But she said..." Johnson's hand went to his pocket and closed around his gun.

"Just what the hell is going on over there?" Hendricks' voice was still calm and deliberate.

"That son-of-a-bitch of a shrink killed Faber?"

Pamela Cook beat a fist on the back of her chair.

"What do I do now, about the shipment? Where is the doctor?" Johnson went on.

"I have just finished talking with the doctor," Hendricks said. "He has my shipment. He has it stashed some place."

"I'll make him talk. He'll tell me where the stuff is."

"You just listen," Hendricks commanded, "I have the doctor's wife here at the office. We are going to make a trade."

"Trade?"

"Doctor Cummins is waiting for you in his hotel room. You get over there now. You have the doctor take you to where he has hidden my shipment. You understand?"

Johnson was nodding his head, listening, his eyes closed.

"First, you get the merchandise, then you take care of that doctor. When that is done, you call me and we'll see what is to be done with his wife. Do you think you can remember that?"

"Yes, sir." Johnson's head was still nodding. "Mr. Hendricks." Johnson's hateful look was on Mary. "I have the doctor's girlfriend with me here."

"Where is here?"

"Pamela Cook's office."

There was a long moment of consideration. "Leave her there till this is taken care of. Cook will know what to do with her. Now you get your ass over to that hotel... and don't fall in the Goddamn pool," Hendricks hung up.

Johnson put the phone down and moved toward Mary. He drew his gun from his pocket and his left hand closed on Mary's throat. The muzzle of the .38 pressed deep into her cheek, below her right eye. Mary made an instinctive move to draw away, but four pair of strong hands held her arms and shoulders.

"Faber is dead." Johnson was inches away from Mary's face, but the words were to Pamela Cook, who was standing behind him. "The doctor killed him at the hotel. That shrink killed Faber." Johnson drove the gun harder into Mary's face.

"That's great. Just what I needed," said Pamela in disgust.

"They found Faber in the hotel pool. Ha didn't take the shipment," Johnson said.

"Where the fuck is it then?" demanded Cook.

"The doctor has it. He is waiting for me at his hotel."

"You dumb ass. You think he will just wait there? Just hand the stuff over to you?" Cook could see her project falling apart.

"He'll wait for me. And he'll hand the stuff over. Hendricks is holding the doctor's wife at the office. We are going to make a trade."

On hearing this, Mary tried desperately to free herself from the many hands holding her. Johnson tightened his fingers on her throat till her fight was gone.

"The doctor will take me to where he has hidden the shipment... then...I'll take care of him." Johnson boasted for Mary's benefit.

"And what are you going to do with her." Cook asked pointedly.

"Hendricks said to leave her here with you for now." Johnson passed on the instructions.

"Thanks a lot... Where the hell can I keep her... This is no God-damn jail."

"I'm only telling you what Hendricks said." Johnson was trying to regain some position.

Pamela Cook walked around her chair and flopped down in it. "You guys are going to blow my cover and ruin two years of work with your fuckin' Starsky and Hutch shit."

Johnson was about to continue the defense of his position, but before he could organize his words, Cook was saying, "Just when I am gearing for the biggest demonstration ever. Two, maybe three hundred people will be there. We'll form a human barricade across the main entrance to the nuclear power plant. There will be little kids there too. Even babies. The police will come down on us with clubs... high pressure hoses, mace. We'll be on every front page and every network newscast in the country." Cook's eyes were burning on Johnson. "So, if you don't want to see this operation come to a screeching halt, you better take care of that doctor, what's his name, and return the shipment... I need my allotment." Cook stood up and leaned over the desk, "This is the first time I have ever been late with my distribution, and my people don't like it... I don't like it." Speech over, she sat back down.

"You'll get your shipment." Johnson assured her. "Now... what are you going to do with her?"

"Lock her in that back storage room for now. I'll find something more permanent later." Looking at Johnson, "We'll have another hostage, in case you blow this job, too." Then to the five women, "Throw her in that storage room."

Mary was gasping for air. The women were on her like the front line of the Steelers. Two had her arms and were tearing at her sleeves. One had yanked the towel from her head and was dragging her by the hair. They shoved Mary through a large door into a storage room at the rear of the building and the last gang-push sent her falling over bundles of books and boxes to the floor. The women slammed the door shut and pulled the bolt, locking it from the outside.

Mary landed hard on her right hip and shoulder. She rolled onto her back and there was a sudden darkness all around her. She lay in that position trying to draw air into her lungs. The choke-hold Johnson put on her had cut off her oxygen and she was fighting back the creeping loss of consciousness. In her mind she was falling away, not like in a dream where you suddenly jolt to reality, but a dream where you keep falling into a long, slow sleep...a dreamless sleep through a tunnel of silent black.

Burt Cummins sat alone in his hotel room. The incredible events of the past twenty-four hours were spinning wildly in his brain. What he had hoped would be a harmless fun/work three days with a beautiful, loving, sexy woman had turned to tragedy. One man was dead. His wife was being held hostage by unknown narcotics peddlers who would have no knowledge or concern for her heart condition, nor care. Mary Parker was probably being held by their Phoenix counterparts. And there was the very strong possibility that it had been Mary who killed the 'fat' man. "Maybe someone else killed Faber," Cummins reasoned. "How could two small banderilla barbs kill a bull-of-a-man that size?... Of course, if she had struck him from behind, and then pushed him into the pool...that would do it."

Cummins, for reasons he could not understand, still could not bring himself to report all this to the police. How could he tell them his wife had been kidnapped, his girlfriend had also been kidnapped. And to pay their ransom he must turn over three bags of pure cocaine he was hiding in his briefcase in a warehouse across town.

His only solution was to turn over the three plastic bags to them. But, how could he be sure the man on the phone would keep his agreement? How could he be sure his wife and Mary would be returned unharmed?

"All Right." Cummins yelled at the empty room. "Send your man. Let him come. But before I give you your Goddamn cocaine.. this is what 'I' want." Cummins was arranging his thoughts for his grandstand speech. "I don't have the stuff here. It's not in this room, and it's not in my car. In fact, it's not at this hotel. I will take you to where it is, but, first I want positive proof that my wife and Mary Parker are safe...and..."

A loud, demanding knock on the door halted his rehearsal. It was time, at last, to come face to face with one of them. Their messenger or their hit-man. Everything depended on how well he could pull this off.

Cummins rose from the bed and went to the door. He grasped the knob with his left hand. A slight pause while he drew a deep nerve settling breath. He swung the door open with a flourish. His right hand raised with jutting index finger an inch away from the man's nose. "Now..."

"Hi. Ready for that drink?"

Burt was standing in the doorway with his finger in the face of the redheaded D.E.A. man. "Have I come at a bad time?" the the red-head asked.

"No, not at all," Burt hurried the words. "I was reading and my mind was miles away."

"If you are not too tired, I thought we might go have that drink. The hotel has a good soft rock group in the lounge, if you like that kind of music."

"I like it fine," Burt said, looking back into the room. "I was sort of expecting a call."

"Tell the desk. They will page you in the lounge."

"I'll get my coat."

Cummins moved back into the room and called the desk and on the way out he took his coat from the back of the chair.

As they walked together along the winding path that led from the rooms to the main lobby of the hotel, Cummins asked, "Any more information on the man they found in the pool?"

"He's not wanted, but he had a rap sheet as long as your arm."

"He did?"

"Don't know yet what he was doing in Phoenix, or who got to him, or why."

"But you are sure it was... murder." Cummins was fishing.

"He didn't stick those things in his back and go off the high board."

"Sounds like a safe bet to me," Cummins agreed, feeling rather foolish and wishing he had never asked the question.

"One thing the lab did come up with that was rather surprising, for a guy that fat and ugly."

"What was that?"

"That guy, just before he died, had sex."

"Sex?"

"The lab found large traces of semen on his pecker, and all fover his shorts. Ain't that the damndest thing you ever heard?"

"You could say that."

When they reached the lounge, and were settled at the bar, the D.E.A. man ordered scotch on the rocks. Cummins ordered a double.

"Double what, sir?" asked the bartnder.

"Double anything," said Cummins, then to himself, 'Mary, Mary. How could you, with that dirty...?' Then he downed his drink.

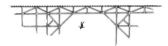

When Mary awoke, it took some hard thinking for her to remember where she was and how she had gotten there. She felt pain in her right side from her hip to her knee. Her shoulder hurt to the elbow and she made an effort to bend her right knee, then a similar test for the right arm. Her mouth and throat were stone dry, and breathing was difficult. Mary forced several deep breaths and gradually the seeming tilt of the room leveled off.

With one arm she managed to roll over, then move to her hands and knees. She groped in the dark for something on which to steady herself. Her hand found the rough wood of a packing crate and she raised herself to a very unsteady standing position. Her eyes had dilated enough to allow her to see the walls of the small room. Three sides were built of plywood and backed with two-by-fours. The rear wall was of cement block and was part of the main building. The plywood walls ran up to the ceiling joists, allowing ten inches between the top of the plywood and the ceiling, and through this gap, the light from the office reflected off the white ceiling. With that much light, and enough time, Mary knew she would be able to see the objects that were strewn across the floor.

Mary's breathing was easier now and her equilibrium was returning. And also was the realization of the danger she was in.

She listened. She could hear voices on the other side of the wall. Women's voices. To hear better, she held her breath and put her ear to the plywood. Mary could not hear Johnson's voice. Only the voices of women. It was possible he had left and was on his way to the hotel and Burt's room. Or he might be there by now. Mary had no way of knowing how long she had been unconscious.

As she strained to hear the conversations on the other side of the plywood wall, one voice came through louder, much louder, than the others.

"Bring me a Coors."

It was Pamela Cook's voice. She sounded far off. Probably sitting at her desk. Mary turnd to survey the room to find a way of escape. She had to get out. She must get to Burt before Johnson did. But how? She might try to rush past them when they came to check on her. That didn't seem like much of a chance and she had no way of knowing when they would come to look in on her, if at all. Maybe she could set fire to the room. Would help arrive in time? Or would she die of smoke inhalation before the fire trucks could get there.

In the back wall, the wall that was part of the cement block building, Mary saw a gray outline. It could be a door, a service entrance. She moved toward the outline, stepping over boxes and bundles of paper. With the help of the reflected light off the ceiling she could read the sign over the wide door. "DOOR MUST REMAIN UNLOCKED DURING BUSINESS HOURS". It was a door. A door like you would find at the rear of any storage building. And like all good storage doors, it would be made of heavy metal. A door with a strong lock.

The wide crash bar, running the width of the door, would be bolted or chained or both. Normally when you put your weight against the bar the door would spring open. When Mary pressed both hands on the crash bar there was a loud metallic clank, and the door swung open. The cool night air rushed in on Mary's face. She could see stars in the cloudless sky. The revolving beam of light from the airport control tower passed over the building. Mary wanted to run, but her legs would not believe her sudden freedom. Her progress was a wobble, a series of stumbles, as if unseen ropes were holding her back. Where would the alley lead? Which way to go? Mary saw a car drive by the open end of the service way. It was a street. A street that she must reach before those inside discovered she had found that door. Two more cars passed left to right and another drove by right to left. Mary moved closer to the street. She was forced to put her hand to the wall of the building to keep from falling. If a car would stop for her, give her a ride to town, find a taxi. Burt would pay the fare when she got to the hotel. But what if Burt and Johnson were on their way to the mini storage and the briefcase?

When Mary reached the street, she had already made up her mind to stop the first car to come by, no matter which direction it might be going.

From far down the street a light was moving toward her. She gave a quick look down the alley. All was dark and all was quiet. As the light came nearer, Mary could see and hear it was a motorcycle. It didn't matter. She would have flagged a kid on a bicycle. Mary moved into the street waving her arms to draw attention to herself. The bike came to a stop in front of her. The rider wore a red leather jacket and a full head helmet with a dark plastic face plate. It hid all possible identification as to whom Mary was asking for help.

"Can you give me a ride?" Mary was yelling over the roar of the motorcycle. "I have to get away from here."

A mumble of sound came from inside the globular helmet and the man motioned with his thumb for Mary to climb on behind him. She swung her leg over the rear seat and settled behind her unseen benefactor, both arms around his middle and the bike sped off, and Mary noticed, away from the airport beacon.

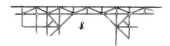

The man from the D.E.A. sat at the bar of the hotel lounge. He held what was left of his fourth scotch at arm's length and studied the glass tumbler, as he turned it slowly in his fingers. "I really can't find any sympathy for that fat guy in the pool," he said to the glass.

Cummins leaned close to hear the words of the redhead. The man was making no effort to have his voice heard over the amplified music emanating from the revolving bandstand. "You see so much of this...sort of thing...it's only natural you become calloused," his speech reflected his four doubles.

"Not a matter of callous," the redhead protested, "Some people get caught up in deals that are not of their making."

"I know what you mean." Cummins was nodding, but his shoulders were moving too, and it was more of a series of bows.

"I feel for them. But, those who profit from the misery of others...those that can close their eyes to the wrecked lives and can only see the money."

"True."

"I don't have a hell of a lot of sympathy for the user either. They know the consequence. They have been told often enough. But, they have to find out for themselves."

"By then it's too late."

"You doctors should try to get to the kids. Talk to them."

"Would they listen?"

There was a long pause, "Mine didn't."

"Yours?"

The D.E.A. man stirred his ice cubes with the tip of his index finger. "My daughter. She was nineteen. Overdose. A party at the university. Sue Ann died before they could get her to a hospital," he downed his scotch.

Cummins sat staring at the multicolored tropical fish swimming in the giant aquarium behind the bar. He could not look at the man at his side. An onrush of guilt filled his stomach and was tying his mind in a knot. How much misery and death was he holding in those three plastic bags? How many lives are to be immolated on his altar structured to worship greed? There was more now than getting his wife and Mary Parker back safely. There was much more. There were hundreds of lives in jeopardy if that cocaine were to be turned over to them...he must move from the defensive to the attack. He was in a position to turn this thing around. The hunted would hunt the hunter. For the first time in his life he felt he had a cause. A cause that was tangible, concrete. He wasn't going to solve the world's drug problems, but by God he could do something about the three plastic bags he was in control of. And, he could start now. Tonight...Could he be sure this was not the liquor just shadow boxing in his mind? Could he bring himself to face the men he would have to face if he were to see this thing through to the end? Burt Cummins hoped he could. Burt Cummins was scared to death that he couldn't.

Cummins saw the bartender moving from person to person along the bar. Seeming to ask a question of each, then move on. When he stopped in front of him, the bartender asked, "Mr. Cummins?"

"I'm Doctor Cummins."

"Call for you in the lobby, sir."

Cummins threw a twenty dollar bill on the bar and as he turned on his stool he said, "That's the call I've been expecting...I'll be right back...if I can."

Before the redhead could answer, if he had intended to answer, Cummins was moving along the row of bar stools on his way to the lobby. He went directly to the desk and asked the clerk, "You have a call for me? I'm Doctor Cummins."

"Yes, Doctor Cummins," the man said, "If you will pick up one of the house-phones." Then pointing into the empty lobby, "They are behind that rock wall. Next to the men's room."

Cummins intended to walk diagonally across the lobby, the shortest distance to the phone, but the four doubles he had consumed in the last hour dictated a 'great circle route.' An inner centrifugal force pushing him slightly off course. Noticing the drift, and his near collision with a couch, he cursed himself for allowing drink to impair his senses with so much at stake, yet knowing if he were sober, he might well be running away.

Picking up the house phone, and bringing it to his ear he hit something metal that was already at his ear.

"Don't move or this gun will take your head off."

Cummins stood with the useless phone in his left hand. The cold muzzle of Johnson's snubnose threateningly pressed at his temple. "O.K.," said Cummins, surprisingly under control, "Your boss told me you would be here. What do we do now?"

"You hand over our merchandise and maybe I won't kill you."

"Nope," said Cummins with a trace of a grin, realizing he had never used the word before in his adult life. "Your boss and I made a deal."

"I don't know nothing about no deal."

"No deal...no merchandise," Cummins gave a cavalier shrug, "Sorry."

"You don't know what sorry is, you shithead," Johnson pulled the hammer back. "You hand over the merchandise now, or your wife and your girlfriend will..."

"I explained to your boss and I'll try to explain to you." Cummins used his most condescending tone. "I don't have the 'merchandise' here. Not on me. Not in my room. Not in my car. Not here in this hotel. I have it...put away. Now, when I know my wife and Mary Parker are safe...then I'll tell you where it is."

"You'll take me to where it is and you'll take me there now."

"I will?"

"Yes, you will," Johnson's voice was shaking with frustration. "If I don't call the office in one hour...your wife will meet with a serious accident...like being burned to death in a fire at your home...your girlfriend's body will be left in the desert...and you will be found floating in the hotel pool."

"That's already been done."

"Look, smart ass," Johnson was becoming desperate. "Think of it as a ticking time bomb. A time bomb set to go off in one hour. A blast that will kill the three of you...and the only way you can prevent it from going off is for me to call the office. So, if I get the merchandise before..."

"What's with this merchandise shit. Can't you say cocaine? Are you so afraid of the word cocaine? Or, didn't your boss man tell you what was in the three little plastic bags? Cocaine, man. Cocaine." Cummins voice was rising. He had never been so voluble in his life. Then he caught sight of the D.E.A. man at the lounge door, he was about to come into the lobby and had stopped to talk with someone for a moment, but he would be moving in a matter of seconds. Could he be on the way to the men's room? Was he checking up on him? Cummins couldn't be seen talking with this man. He had to move now. "Come on, I'll take you to where I have hidden your cocaine," Cummins blurtd out. "And put that damn gun away before you blow the deal for everyone." Cummins turned and walked to the far end of the stone wall and the stunned Johnson lowered his gun and followed him through the large double doors leading to the pool and to room 212.

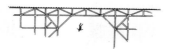

Mary Parker was hugging the motorcyclist around the waist with both arms as they sped down a dark Phoenix street. His helmet did little to deflect the wind and Mary's damp hair was being whipped into knots that formed a crazy web of dark lines across her face. Squinting through watering eys she saw the electric sign of an all-night 7/ll store.

"If you will stop at that store, I can use the phone." Mary was yelling into the side of the helmet. The rider gave a nod and throttled back. Feathering the brakes lightly with his right hand, he made a smooth turn into the well-lighted parking lot of the 7/ll store and came to a stop before a row of telephones.

Mary was swinging her leg over the bike, but still holding on to the biker's shoulders for balance. The biker turned the ignition key and the motor stilled. After removing his heavy black gloves, he lifted the sphere helmet. For the first time Mary could see the face of the man who had come to her aid. He had short blond hair topping a trim six foot frame and a face that could sell Arrow shirts. His age not over thirty.

"I'm sorry," Mary said, turning back to the biker. "I don't have my purse and I need a dime to call my hotel."

"In this town you need twenty cents." The man reached into his tight biker pants and brought out a fistful of change. "Take what you need," he smiled.

Mary picked a dime and two nickels from his hand. "I'll pay you back, and for the ride, too. I'm very grateful."

Mary went to the middle stall attached to the side of the building. Her first problem was to find the number of the Mountain Shadows Hotel. Finding that, she was told Dr. Cummins had received a phone call and had left the hotel. At least he was not in his room and he did not answer the page. Mary hung the phone back on the hook. Johnson had beaten her to the hotel and he and Burt were probably on their way to the mini storage building by now.

"Could I ask one more favor?" Mary said as she returned to the biker.

"Try," he answered.

"1620 East Camelback Road. Could you take me there? It's very important." Mary's eyes pleaded as her hands tried to push the tangled hair from her face.

"I think I can manage that. Climb on."

Once again Mary swung her leg over the rear saddle and put her arms around the rider's waist. A turn of the key brought the engine to life and the Honda Goldwing glided into the night.

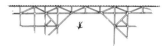

Doctor Cummins walked directly to where his Mark VI was parked. Johnson followed close behind. When Cummins turned to enter his Lincoln, Johnson drew his .38 and called, "Not your car, Doctor. Over here," indicating the black Datsun parked on the far side of the parking lot. Cummins then walked silently to the passenger side of the little car. "Hold it," Johnson ordered. "This side. You drive."

Cummins came around the car and Johnson opened the door and stepped back. "Get in."

Cummins bent into the driver's seat and sat behind the wheel. Johnson slammed the door with his left hand, his right kept the gun aimed at Cummins' head.

While Johnson walked back to the passenger side, Cummins was trying to remember the address of the mini storage. His still slightly inebriated mind was ready to take a short cut and had almost ordered his left hand to reach for his wallet with the business card that had the address on one side and the combination on the other. His motion froze before it had begun. His first tinge of fear. Fear in the knowledge that if this man saw the card, or evey suspected he had such information on him, he would surely be killed...and so would his wife and Mary. He had to force his memory to recall the street and number. If he could only remember the half page ad in the Yellow Pages, to redisplay the image in his mind. It said, "You Lock And You Keep The Key".Below that, he remembered, was the telephone number...he sure as hell didn't need that. The street? It was Camel...Camelback Road...East Camelback Road. That was it. But, where on Camelback Road? How do I get from here to Camelback? Can't be north. There is desert and mountains to the north. It is south. O.K. it's south from here on East Camelback Road. If he could find that little French restaurant...he could go on from there.

Johnson climbed into the car and as he closed his door, he was saying, "Let's go." Cummins held out his hand, palm up.

"The key?" he asked calmly

"In the ignition."

"Naughty, naughty," chided Cummins as he started the car. "With the type of people we have around here lately, it is dangerous to leave keys in a car."

"Just shut your mouth and drive...you do know where you're going?" Johnson asked sarcastically.

"I'm trying to remember." Cummins hoped he had made the truth sound facetious. He then pulled out onto Lincoln Drive and moved west...looking for some landmark that might give him a clue to where he was going. "This desert looks different by moonlight," Cummins murmured to himself.

"What was that?"

"I said the moon makes the desert look peaceful."

"You keep driving to wherever it is you're goin' or you will become part of this real estate."

Cummins drove for several minutes, still searching for some recognizable street or sign. Then, and only for a split second, he saw the moonlight reflect on something metal, something shining. It seemed to be suspended over a house. It was the crossarms of a radio antenna. The antenna over Senator Barry Goldwater's shack. Cummins now knew he was driving in the right direction, at least.

Topping the next rise he could see a blanket of twinkling lights covering the valley below. Far off, to what seemed to be the center of town, Cummins saw the spinning white and green beacon at the Phoenix Airport. He had passed that on the way into town. When he came to where Lincoln Drive divided with one lane turning left and the other straight ahead, Cummins took the left lane and followed the long banked curve taking him down a gentle slope into the valley. A sign on his left read, Arizona Biltmore, he remembered that, too. Saks Fifth Avenue. Mary had mentioned she wanted to do some shopping there.

The headlights reflected on a large sign with white letters, CAMELBACK ROAD. He pressed the accelerator and made a left turn as the green arrow turned to red. He had been heading south so a left turn would put him driving east. East on Camelback. There was little traffic on the wide street and he had no trouble moving to the far lane. As was his habit, Cummins checked his mirror to be sure the lane was clear, and it was, but in the mirror he could see a large sign, in reverse. It took little effort to flip-flop the letters and read, 'Cafe Casino.' The little French restaurant was dropping back fast. He was going east on Camelback Road, but away from the mini storage building.

"How the hell do I turn around without this creep knowing I'm lost?" he asked himself.

Cummins kept driving. He was nearly sober now.

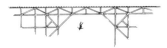

Mary had no way of knowing the black Datsun making a right turn in front of her at the corner of 24th Street and Camelback Road carried Cummins and Johnson. At that moment she was more concerned with holding both arms tightly around the biker and pressing her thighs against his rump as he expertly leaned the Honda into a smooth turn to head west on Camelback Road.

"It's the mini storage on your left," Mary shouted after they had gone a few blocks.

The mini storage sign could be seen in the pale blue light afforded by the mercury vapor street lamps from high on their poles. The Honda backed off the power as they reached the driveway and coasted into the dark, narrow streets of the storage complex.

When the bike came to a stop, Mary swung her left leg over the rear seat and stood by the biker as if dismissing a taxi or chauffer.

"If you will give me your name and address, I would like to send you a check for all your trouble," Mary said.

"No trouble," said the biker.

"I'd like to, just the same."

"That won't be ncessary. I'm glad I could help...if I did."

"You certainly did. You may have saved my life."

"O.K. Forget the check and send a medal," the biker grinned.

Mary stole a quick look up the alleyway expecting any second to see the white Lincoln.

"You have been most helpful," Mary said, still looking away. "I'll be all right now. I've taken too much of your time already."

"I don't like to leave you here alone." The biker seemed truly concerned.

"They will be along soon. They are late now, but they'll be here."
Mary's words were meant to be reasurring, but her tone was a contradiction.

"I don't mind waiting," and the biker put his kickstand down and pulled his leg over the bike so he was sitting sidsaddle facing Mary. He took a pack of cigarettes from the zipper pocket of his jacket and offered one to Mary. She shook her head. While he lit his cigarette, Mary noticed books bunjied to the rear of the motorcycle. "Are you a student?" she asked.

"I am what is known as a professional student," and he made little quotation marks with bent fingers to bracket the word professional. "Have been for twenty years."

"I had to take my senior year over, but twenty years."

"Counting kindergarten, grade school, high school and four years of college, makes seventeen. And I spent three years graduate studies in music. The family wanted me to be a concert musician. Piano. Anton Rubinstein, Paderewski and Horowitz. Of course, I never came close."

"I took piano and ballet for three years, but it doesn't show." Mary admitted. "Do you come from a musical family?"

"Not really. My grandfather was the last 'stand by' organist in radio."

Mary wanted to say, "That's nice," and perhaps end the conversation, but instead she was asking, "What is a 'stand by' organist?"

"In the early days of radio, as grandfather told me, every large radio station had their 'stand by' organist. His job was to stay in the studio all day and when something went wrong, when they had 'dead-air,' the announcer would cup one hand over his ear and say, 'AND NOW, WITH GEORGE WEAVER AT THE CONSOLE OF THE MIGHTY WURLITZER, WE PRESENT A SHORT MUSICAL INTERLUDE.' They would then open the microphone in the studio and grandad would keep playing till the 'ON AIR' light went out."

"Sounds boring," Mary said.

"He also played for daytime soap operas. That was fun, he said. Then the shows all moved to New York and Hollywood and granddad moved here to Phoenix. His last job, before he died, was playing organ in a local pizza parlor. He hated the job, but loved the instrument. Not a small Hammond, but a powerful pipe organ. Four manuals, dozens of stops, six expression pedals. The organ had been in the orchestra pit of a large west coast theatre and was rescued just before the building

120

was to be torn down. They had to make way for a parking lot." The biker folded his arms across his chest as he thought back to his early years in music. "I would stay with grandad after the pizza parlor closed and we would play Bach and Handel. There is a tremendous feeling of power with an organ of that size. All the tonal colors of a full symphony orchestra at your fingertips...and loud? We could break windows a block away." The biker drew deeply on his cigarette and blew a long trail of smoke. "Grandad was a wonderfully talented musician, plus a teacher and a friend... I tried very hard to become what he would have liked me to have been. To play in all the famous churches in the world. All the great theatres and music halls...But I found the concert field was very uncertain and I didn't want to end up playing 'I Left My Heart In San Francisco' five times a night for a bunch of musically illiterata pizza eaters...so I went back to school."

"Back to college?" Mary asked.

"Seminary. I studied for the pristhood."

"You are a priest?" Mary blurted.

"No. In my second year I dropped out. A few things I couldn't hack."

"Like?"

The biker considered his answer for a long moment.

"I lost my belief in God."

"There's not much call for priests who don't believe in God."

"I believe in 'a' God. My trouble was in believing in the God as presented in the Bible. In Christ. Do you know what I mean?" The man's eyes were pleading for understanding.

"I'm sorry, but no, I don't." Mary was not abrupt but definite. "Why would anyone spend even two years if they had this lack of belief, of faith?"

"It came on me rather suddenly. I'm not at all proud of it." The biker could not look Mary in the eye. "But you don't want to hear..."

"Yes, I would." Mary cut in. "I would very much like to hear."

"I was a fake, going to the seminary in the first place," he began. "When it looked like I might be drafted, I started thinking of being a priest."

"Priests go to war. I have an uncle who was an army chaplain. He wasn't a priest, but he told me there were a lot of priests that were chaplains in the war."

"You must understand, I was playing for time... After you are ordained you can become a chaplain... but that takes twelve years. I figured by the time twelve years went by, the whole thing would be over..."

"Wouldn't it have been easier just to go to Canada?"

"No. Ever since I was a kid...altar boy and all that stuff, I thought being a priest would be a good thing, a good life. To be able to help other people. Sure, we were all looking for ways to beat the draft... I was doing well at the seminary...then one day I got a telegram...my older brother had been killed in Vietnam. Killed trying to save the life of a buddy... Didn't he die for our sins? My brother didn't have any assurance or promise that in three days he would rise again. Not only Jim, but thousands of other GI's. Did they?"

"So what are you trying to prove?"

"It proves it's no big deal to give up your life for three days. Lady, I've been drunk for longer than that. It is when you don't know for sure you are going to rise on that third day... When you don't know for sure that there is even a heaven. That is the real sacrifice. Those are the ones that give up their lives."

Mary didn't speak for several seconds. "I guess it's a matter of faith. You have it or you don't. Simple as that."

"What is there left to have faith in. Faith in God? What God?... If there was a God of nature...I'd maybe go for that God. You can't have faith in man. Man's abuse of his fellow man, both social and political. His vice and greed. The enslavement of people since time began... They have caused want and misery... These evils are taken now as natural, expected and unavoidable... But nature...planets keep to their appointed paths and never deviate from them. Nature is orderly, lawful, rational and predictable... Man has ignored the natural laws, laws of society and the laws of God."

"All I know is that an awful lot of people don't think they believe in God until they are about to die. Then it's a whole new ball game." Mary was trying to lighten the conversation and end it, if possible.

"Death is not that big a deal either. Nobody wants to die. To shorten their life. But look at it this way. There are only two ways about it. You are alive or you are dead. For millions of years, when dinosaurs roamed through the swamps, when the ancient Egyptians built their pyramids and the Sphinx. You were dead all those thousands of years. You have been dead a lot longer than you have been alive. Being dead should be nothing new to us."

"When you are born, God gives you a soul. Then you are alive and for the first time." Mary tried to explain.

122

The man on the bike looked at Mary and then looked away in deep thought. "You might just have something... The soul makes the difference. I'll have to do some thinking on that."

This man was beginning to talk like a kook. Yet, there she was listening to his life story and she didn't even know his name. Not that she cared...his report on his lack of faith was becoming frightening. She would try one more time.

"I want to thank you for all your help getting me here. My boss is coming any minute and I don't think it would be a good idea if he saw me here with a...stranger. You know what I mean?"

"No, I don't, but I know what you are saying, so I'll be on my way." He flicked his cigarette making a golden pinwheel in the dark. "You're sure you will be all right?"

"I'm sure."

"O.K. Whatever you say. It was nice talking with you." The rider swung his leg over the bike and turned the key and the strong sound of the engine filled the night. "Be careful," he warned as he was speeding away.

"Thanks again," Mary called after him. She wished she hadn't been so rude, but she had become frightened by his conversation. Mary watched him glide into the street, then he was lost behind the building. She was now alone. She retreated into the shadows. If only she could remember which storage space held the briefcase. It was on the right, that much she remembered. If she could stay hidden, tight up against the steel storage doors and wait until Burt drove in, she would follow them. Then she would... 'Then she would what?' What will I be able to do? That guy will have his gun. Maybe I can find a piece of pipe... Oh, where is Burt? It shouldn't take this long from the hotel to here. What's happened to him?

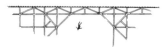

Cummins had known for the last ten minutes he was driving in the wrong direction, away from the mini storage. Making a right turn off Camelback Road he saw a sign that read 'YOU ARE LEAVING PHOENIX ADIOS AMIGOS' When he made a second right turn, a street sign read 'YOU ARE LEAVING SCOTTSDALE WELCOME TO PHOENIX'

"That's the second time you've turned right," Johnson shoved his gun against Cummins' ribs. "You're driving in circles."

"I only know one way to get there and this is the way. If you don't like it...you drive."

"You're heading back the way we came..." Johnson gave a quick look into the night. "What the hell street is this?"

"Sign said Indian School Road. I'm looking for 24th Street...I don't want this to come as a shock to you, but when we get there I'm going to turn right again."

"I don't know what you're trying to pull, but if we aren't there in five minutes, you're a dead man. Now move it."

"Whatever you say, but your boss is going to be mad as hell if you don't stick to our bargain...cause you get nothing until I know my wife and Mary are safe... That's the deal."

"You find the place and show me the stuff, then we'll talk about the deal."

Cummins drove looking straight ahead. "We just crossed 28th Street...Four more blocks."

"You get off this Goddamn merry-go-round or you'll end up face down in the gutter."

Cummins made no answer. His mind was now working ahead to what he would do at the mini storage. If he couldn't remember the address, he sure as hell couldn't remember the combination.

As he neared 24th Street, he slowed to give the signal light time to go from red to green. When the light changed, he pressed the gas pedal and made a right turn. Out of the corner of his eye he could see Johnson's reaction.

"You turn that wheel right one more time, even to avoid hitting something, and I'm going to blow you away. You got that?"

"At the next light I will turn left. That should make you happy."

The closer Cummins came to the mini storage the more worried he became. He would have to take out the card and read the combination. If Johnson was going to use the gun...that would be the time...when he had everything set in front of him.

The signal changed from red to a green left-turn arrow and Cummins turned west on Camelback.

When Cummins gave a look into his mirror, he was surprised to see a police car close behind. He was sure Johnson hadn't seen the car...if he hit his brakes suddenly, the police might ram into him... Cummins thought about turning off his lights, driving without lights deserves a ticket... Before he could decide which violation to commit, the police car had swung to his right and was passing him. For a second he pressed on the gas, but the pressure of Johnson's gun in his side changed his mind.

Cummins had to look hard to see the sign because of the dim street lights.

"Here we are," Cummins said. The Datsun pulled into the storage area and moved to the far alley. They slowed to less than five miles an hour. If he was in the correct alleyway, the storage would be on his right. Maybe he should stop and walk and see which doors had the combination locks. Then Cummins saw 207. That was it. He remembered seeing the little old man with the big nose and the black bushy eyebrows print 'VANTAGE' across the plastic sheet over number 207. The Datsun came to a stop.

"Is this it?" Johnson asked.

"Yeah."

"Which one?"

"I'll show you."

Johnson kept his gun on Cummins as they both moved out of the car. "Which one?" demanded Johnson.

"Behind you."

Johnson turned to stare at the heavy steel garage door and the big number 207. "O.K. Open it. Get over here and open the Goddamn door."

Cummins moved around the car and up to the lock that hung from the hasp. "I'm trying to remember the combination."

"Get back," said Johnson. "I'll shoot the damn thing off."

"And wake up the whole neighborhood? You shoot the lock...or me...or both, and while you are looking to see which box it's in...the police will be all over you."

"What do you mean...which box?"

"There are hundreds of boxes in that room...and the stuff is in one of them."

"Open the Goddamn lock."

Cummins wet the tips of his fingers with his tongue and tried a few turns of the knob. Then he wet the tips again and rubbed them hard on his coat sleeve, like a movie safecracker using an emery board. He made a few more turns of the knob and tilted his head, as if listening for the sound of tumblers.

"What the hell are you doing?" Johnson finally demanded.

"I'm trying to open this lock. It's a tough one."

"Look doctor," Johnson placed his gun to the back of Cummins' head. "If I lose my patience...your patients are going to lose their doctor...now find the combination and open that fuckin' lock."

"I could have remembered, if you had just waited a minute." Cummins drew his wallet from his pocket and took out the card. He spun the dial to zero, then followed the directions and in a moment the lock fell open.

"Get back," ordered Johnson as he moved up and took the handle and raised the door full open. He looked into the dark room. "Where's the light?"

"On the wall to your left," Cummins answered numbly, knowing he had reached the end of the charade. He had run out of delaying tactics.

The light switch clicked and a single bulb hanging from the ceiling filled the room with a harsh white light. Johnson looked into the seemingly empty room. He soon saw the brown leather briefcase alone in the far corner.

"Hundreds of boxes?" Johnson almost laughed. "Hundreds of boxes my ass."

Johnson again pointed the .38 at Cummins. "Bring it here," he demanded.

Burt Cummins had missed his chance to run. Every instinct told him to run. To run into the darkness. To hide until this killer with a gun went away with his 'shipment,' but instead, he stood stone still. Made no move. His eyes steady on the briefcase. In his mind he could see the three plastic bags that had changed his life, and perhaps would kill him. And he was surprised he was not afraid. He was the young bullfighter testing one bull too many.

"I said bring it here," Johnson's voice brought Cummins back and he moved forward, picked up the briefcase and carried it in his arms. "Come on, damn it. Don't take all night."

"Open the case," Johnson said with the excitement of a child waiting to see the gifts Santa had brought.

Cummins turned the three brass wheels on the face of the lock and clicked the latch open. He was giving this man the three bags of misery and death. Slowly he raised the cover of the briefcase. Johnson could see the three green plastic bags. His breathing became heavy, his job was nearly finished. He would have returned Hendrick's merchandise.

"Close it," Johnson ordered and took a half step back. His gun all the while level at Cummins' middle.

"Hand me the case," Johnson said softly and Cummins handed the briefcase to him. Johnson put the case under his arm and held his gun out threateningly in Cummins' face.

"No, back up, damn you. Back up." Johnson was shouting now. "All the way back."

Cummins was retreating one small step at a time. Was this the way it was going to end? Killed by a stupid jerk of a gunman? There was no balance. Why couldn't he die in an effort to destroy the cocaine. One final act that would give a reason to his life. Was there any justification in not risking all to save the life of Martha or Mary? Still Cummins was backing slowly.

"What about the deal?" Cummins asked. "The deal with your boss."

"Fuck the deal," Johnson sneered. "You've been jackin' me

around all night. Well, I don't need you any more. By the time they find your body, I'll be long gone. You've been a pain in the ass, but you won't be any more. Not for me, not for anybody.'' Johnson straightened his right arm to fire.

"You'll need the keys to the Datsun," Cummins said calmly.

Johnson's right arm slacked slightly, "Keys?"

"I have the keys. If you shoot me, then have to look..."

"Nice try, very nice. But I have a second set of keys."

Johnson was staring hard at Cummins. His gun was pointing directly at Cummins' heart. His finger was full around the trigger and squeezing.

Cummins closed his eyes. As if in prayer, he was saying, "Martha, please forgive me. I'm sorry, I'm sorry. Please forgive me..." He braced himself for the bullet that would tear through his body. He waited. Then he heard a thud, a grunt, and the sound of what could be a gun hitting the cement floor.

Cummins forced his eyes open. There, where Johnson had stood a moment before, Mary was standing. In her hands she held a large brick. One corner soaked red with blood. Crumpled at her feet was Johnson.

"Mary," Cummins moved toward her, "Oh, my God. How did you...? How did you get here? What have they done to you?" The questions came tumbling out.

"Do you think he's dead?" Mary asked looking down on Johnson's body.

"He could be. Hitting him with that brick"

"It was all I could find." Mary shut her eyes tightly to blot out the scene and tears formed as she turned away.

"Don't worry about it. You saved my life. He was going to kill me. Another second...two at the most." Cummins was hazy headed trying to sort out the events of the last twenty seconds. Trying to separate what actually happened. "Mary, I don't know how you did it. How did you find me?"

"They had me locked up in some building. But I found a door and ran." Mary made a shrugging motion with her shoulders. "I heard him say," indicating Johnson lying at her feet, "he would make you take him to where the 'stuff' was and I just..." and she shrugged her shoulders again.

"Anyway, you did it."

"What do we do with him?" The shock of it all was beginning to get to Mary and she seemed a little faint, and she thought she might be sick.

"Leave him right here," Cummins said, "By the time they find him we'll have this all settled."

"Are you sure, Burt?" Tears were heavy on both cheeks, "This is my second one tonight."

"So I heard." Burt moved toward her, "But let's hurry. Keep the brick for now. Fingerprints, you know. I'll throw it away later." Cummins bent over and took both feet by the heels and pulled Johnson's body to the center of the storage room. A trail of blood flowed onto the floor. Cummins picked up Johnson's gun and stuck it in his waistband, then began searching the coat pockets and brought out some papers.

"Burt, what are you doing?" Mary gasped in surprise at his macbre actions.

"Never know how much information you can find in a man's pockets." He pulled a black leather wallet from Johnson's back pocket.

When Cummins thought he had found all there was to find, he stood up and moved to Mary and took the bloody brick from her. "Get in the car. I'll turn off the light and lock the door."

Mary walked into the darkness of the alleyway while Cummins turned out the light, picked up the briefcase and pulled the door down and set the lock, being careful to wipe away his fingerprints.

Just before Mary reached the car, she turned, "What about the keys?"

"I left them in the ignition."

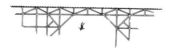

Cummins and Mary Parker drove the Datsun until they found an all night convenience market. After wiping every surface of the interior and door handles with a handkerchif, they abandoned the car in the parking lot and took a Yellow Cab back to the hotel. On the way, Burt asked the driver to stop on an irrigation canal bridge.

"Irrigation canal?" questioned the driver.

"If you would please." said Cummins.

"I'll go up Sixteenth Street. There is a canal just before Indian School Road."

On the bridge the driver stopped at the curb.

"Thanks, I'll only be a moment," Cummins said as he backed out of the taxi concealing the blood stained brick behind him.

The puzzled cab driver lined up Mary's face in his rear-view mirror. "What's your friend up to, miss?"

"It is silly," Mary mumbled, "but we put a love note in a bottle. We want to drop it in the canal and see how far it will travel across the desert."

The driver gave a gruff laugh and with an exaggeratd manipulation of his tongue, he shifted the cigar stub to the other side of his mouth. "It sure as hell won't travel very damn far tonight. Them canals are dried up. Will be for a week. Some sort of repair work."

Mary stiffled a laugh with a cupped hand as Cummins returned to the cab. "Thank you driver," said Cummins as he settled back in the seat next to Mary. "Mountain Shadows Hotel, please."

Mary's laughter was now uncontrollable and she leaned against Burt's shoulder. "The canal...is dry," she managed to say. "No water in it... It is being repaired."

"I thought it was strange. I didn't hear a splash." And they both laughed and held each other very tightly. It was the first laugh they had shared in two days.

In the hotel room, Cummins had spread all the articles he had taken from Johnson's pockets on the small table. Two Western Airlines boarding passes, driver's license, social security card, a business card from Hendricks and Cooper, address 2424 Pearl, Beverly Hills. A white 3x4 file card with a hand drawn map showing the route from the Mountain Shadows Hotel to an address in south Phoenix, with the word COOK. A sheet of typewriter paper with a larger map, presumably drawn by the same person, with a starting point at Mountain Shadows, through Blyth, and on to the Santa Monica Freeway. The initials H and C were in a red circle in Beverly Hills at the intersection of Cannon and Pearl. There was seventy-six dollars in small bills. The last piece was a printed folder announcing the Southwestern States Seminar for the study psychology in the urban society. On its cover was a flattering picture of Dr. Burton Cummins, taken several years ago.

As Cummins began to review the material a third time, Mary came from the bathroom wearing a deep rose mini night-shirt, V necked, short sleeves and a shirt-tail bottom. She moved across the room and silently sat on the edge of the bed facing Burt. She watched him as he read the papers and cards for several minutes.

"Find anything?" she finally asked.

"I think I have," Burt put down the larger map and picked up the driver's license. "His name is Johnson. Robert Johnson. Lived in Los Angeles." He put the license on the table and picked up the 3x4 file card. "This is a map. It shows a place in south Phoenix. Has the name Cook on the bottom." Cummins turned to Mary. "Cook? Isn't that the woman you told me about? The one who had you locked up?"

"That bitch."

"This Cook, she doesn't know about this, Johnson, yet."

"Nobody does, I hope."

"She isn't going to volunteer the information that she let you get away. Not for a while."

Mary gave another, 'I guess so,' shrug.

Cummins was formulating a plan from the information on the table before him, but not yet sure what the final action would be and not at all sure that it would succeed when he found it.

"This card," Cummins held up the business card of Hendricks and Cooper, "and this map with the letters H and C. That is their headquarters. That is where they are holding Martha. It must be."

"What can we do?"

"The man who phoned me, he's the one. He's the one calling the shots. If I could get to him. If I could get to talk to him."

"Hendricks. That was it. Hendricks." Suddenly Mary's eyes were wide open. "The guy Johnson called from Cook's office. His name was Hendricks, I'm sure of it."

"Was there anything else?"

"From what I could hear of the conversation, Johnson was to 'take care of you'."

"He damn near did."

"Johnson was to call Hendricks when he had the stuff and then drive back to Los Angeles."

"Can you remember if anything was said about a deadline or time limit?" Burt asked.

"No, I don't think so."

"Johnson must have thrown that in on his own. Anything else? Anything at all?" Burt urged.

"That they were holding your wife hostage and they would force you to give them the cocaine." Mary was in tears now, "I'm sure the name was Hendricks."

"I must talk to this Hendricks." Burt began to pace the room.

"You can't talk to him," snapped Mary. "Johnson is supposed to have...taken care of you."

"What the hell am I going to do?"

"Let me call," Mary suggested.

"You? Why you?"

"Not me as me, but, I make the call pretending to be one of Cook's workers. She has a lot of them."

Cummins went to the chair by the patio window and sat down. "What good would it do?" He looked down at the papers and cards on the table. "I better call the Los Angeles Police and tell them the whole story. Tell them where they are holding Martha."

"You don't know for sure she is being held at their office."

"I have to do something."

"We might buy some time."

Cummins sat very still. He was exploring all possible avenues and there seemed to be only one that might work, and that was a long shot. He handed Hendricks' business card to Mary. "Dial 9 for an outside line."

Mary dialed the numbers and let it ring. After the third ring there was a click, music began...like an answering machine was on the line. A thin voice said, "Thank you for calling Hendricks and Cooper. Our office hours are nine to five, Monday through Friday. If you wish to make an appointment with one of our talent advisors, please give your name and telephone number and if you want help in motion-pictures, commercial television or in music. You will have twenty seconds to state your message after the tone..." As the tone sounded Mary hung up the phone.

"What was it, Mary? What was it?" Burt asked.

"Just a recorded message. They run some sort of entertainment company. For actors and singers... That is about all I got out of it." Mary looked at the card again and turned it over, as if putting the face away and out of sight.

"Burt," she said, holding the card up close to examinee the reverse side. "There is a number on the back. A telephone number."

Burt took the card from Mary and looked at the numbers scrawled on the back.

"Why didn't I see that?" Burt complained.

"Let me call," Mary urged.

"It may be nothing," Burt did not want to let his hopes get out of rein. "People are always making notes on back of cards and matchbook covers." He handed the card to Mary. "Give it a try."

"This time Mary dialed the numbers with great care." The 9 for an outside line, the area code 213, then the numbers. She could hear the clicks and buzzes as the relays at the phone company did their thing to match up the phones, then the phone was ringing. "It's ringing," Mary whispered and Burt nodded his head. She swallowed as she felt her mouth going dry, and tried to wet her lips.

"Hello." a man's voice answered.

"Mr. Hendricks, please."

"This is Hendricks."

"I'm calling for Mr. Robert Johnson and Miss Cook." Mary was beginning to doubt she could get by with the impersonation.

"Who is this? How did you get this number?"

"I work for Miss Cook here in Phoenix," Mary was drawing a blank. She didn't know what she wanted to say but she just kept talking. "I have a message for you from Mr. Johnson. Said it had to get to you tonight."

"Why can't Johnson make his own call?"

Mary closed her eyes to shut out everything and tried to concentrate on a story.

"Mr. Johnson said he could not get to a phone safely. Not yet. He said to tell you he had taken care of the doctor and Cook would take care of the girl."

"And my shipment? What about my shipment?"

"Johnson has it and he said not to do anything to the doctor's wife until he talks with you. Very important."

"What the hell are you talking about?" Hendricks was becoming wary.

"Johnson said to tell you the doctor had some very heavy connections and she might know something about them. That's all he said."

"That son-of-a-bitch is up to something, and I don't like it."

"There was one more thing," Mary's mind was spinning now. "Mr. Johnson said he hadn't had any sleep for three days and when he had everything safely across the state line...he was going to get some sleep."

"Sleep?" Hendricks yelled into the phone.

"It was Miss Cook's suggestion. She said she didn't want Mr. Johnson falling asleep at the wheel and have an accident. Not with the three plastic bags in the car. She said you would understand."

"She did? Well, I don't. I don't understand at all." Hendricks' voice was becoming louder with each word. "Johnson is up to something and I'm going to find out what it is," and Hendricks slammed the phone down.

Mary sat on the edge of the bed with the phone pressed to her forehead. Tears coming to her eyes, and Cummins moved to her side and took her in his arms.

"Mary, you were wonderful. I don't know how you did it."

"Do you think he believed me?" she was sobbing now. "What if he calls Cook? He'll know it was a trick. Burt, I'm so scared."

"What was that part about 'sleep,' what was that for?"

"For you." Mary said simply. "I knew you couldn't go much longer without sleep. It was to buy some time." Mary put her head against Burt's shoulder. "So was the thing about the 'heavy connections.' I saw it work on television. After the third 'by the way,' Columbo told the killers their hostage had some important information. He figured they wouldn't hurt the girl until they found the information. There really wasn't any information and it gave Columbo the time needed to catch the killers."

"Mary, you are unbelieveable. Wonderful and unbelieveable."

He kissed the top of her head and held her close until they both fell asleep.

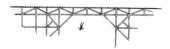

It was five minutes before six the next morning when Carlos Juarado arrived with four other bellman to begin the day shift at the Mountain Shadows Hotel. He was waiting by the time-clock at the employees entrance for the night shift to punch out.

"Hey mon." A co-worker who was going off duty called to Carlos, "You should have stayed on the night shift. You miss all the excitement."

"No way, Jose," smiled Carlos. "I got lovely wetback woman home. Don't worry about my excitement."

The friend did a little rhumba dance and struck the timeclock on the beat. "They took a drunk out of the pool last night."

"I remember a night we didn't take a drunk out of the pool. That was excitement." Carlos looked to his friends for their reaction to his joke.

"Naw. This guy was dead. Had all his clothes on and everything...and guess what. Sticking out of his back was two banderillas. Real ones."

"Banderillas?" Carlos repeated thoughtfully.

"And just an hour ago they find a guy dead in the cactus out behind wing D. Some guy who work for Jack Ross. I tell you, mon, some wild night."

"I'm happy I was not here..." Carlos punched his timecard and before putting the card back in the rack, "Seems to me I saw a pair of banderillas here yesterday... or the day before. I can't remember where I saw them, but I do remember thinking... 'What she doing with banderillas?' It was a woman. That I remember."

"You ought to go tell the police," his friend advised.

"I go talking to the police they might take away my green card. The guy who sold it to me said don't let nobody see it if you don't have to. They would have me hopping bells at the Juarez Hilton for the rest of my life. No thanks. I don't remember nothing." And he went on to work.

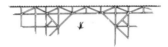

A loud knocking on the door woke Burt Cummins from a deep sleep. He was still wearing his shirt and pants. Mary was asleep beside him, and her mini nightshirt was pulled up to her armpits. Burt's left hand rested lightly on her right breast. The nipple standing hard between his kneading fingers. His face snuggled, lovingly against her left breast. The patio drapes had been drawn tight and the room was in near darkness, even though outside the April sun was beginning to warm the valley. Burt listened, wondering if he had been awakened by someone at the door, or if he had heard the knock in a nervous dream. Then it came again. Five separate, strong knocks. Burt rolled out of bed and threw the sheet over Mary. She stirred in her sleep and turned on to her stomach.

Going to the door, Cummins ran his fingers through his uncombed hair in an attempt to bring some sort of order to his appearance...then his right hand made a quick check of his fly... with Mary, he could never be sure.

When Cummins opened the door, he was again facing Vince Reed, the D.E.A. man, the man with the red hair. The man he had left at the bar the night before...and the night before seemed a month ago.

"Morning doctor," was the red head's greeting.

"Morning," Burt held back a yawn.

"Get you up too early?"

"Not really," Burt looked down at his badly wrinkled pants and shirt. "I fell asleep, watching telvision." Then, selfconsciously, "What time is it?"

"Ten to seven." Vince Reed looked from side to side, as if to see if anyone could overhear their conversation. "Is there someplace where we can talk?" His tone becoming serious.

"Talk?" Cummins questioned.

"I wouldn't disturb you if it weren't business."

"Yours or mine?"

"Mine, I'm afraid. Will you join me by the pool? I'll order the coffee."

"Give me five minutes."

Cummins took a quick shower, shaved and put on fresh underwear, brown slacks and shoes, a tan open neck sport shirt. He was putting his wallet, keys and change in his pants pocket when Mary sat up in bed.

"Where are you going?" she asked sleepily.

"I have to talk to a man."

"What man?"

"A police-man."

"Police?"

"Nothing to worry about," Burt reassured her. "He wants to talk about something that has nothing to do with us."

"If he has nothing to do with us, why...?"

"He is a friend of mine. Everything is all right."

"You're sure?"

"I'm sure. Now, if you will get up and get dressed. We have a long way to go and a lot to do when we get there." Burt leaned over the bed and kissed Mary's cheek. "When you are dressed, take all those papers of Johnson's, tear them up and flush them down the toilet. Maybe you should do it before you get dressed."

"What about the wallet?" Mary asked.

"I'll get rid of that later."

"Keep the keys and the gun of course."

Vince Reed was sitting at a glass-top, poolside table under a wide yellow umbrella that protected him from the brilliant morning sun. On the table in front of him were two cups and a large silver coffee server. Beside the D.E.A. man's cup was his dogeared, spiral notebook and a stub of a pencil.

"Cream and sugar?" Reed asked as he filled Burt's cup with steaming coffee.

"Black, please." Cummins sat down.

"I don't like to bring up such unpleasantness so early," Reed began apologetically.

"Unpleasantness?"

"Last night a scurity guard reported a floodlight burned out in the cactus garden behind your room."

"Yes..."

"When the hotel maintenance man went into the cactus garden to replace the floodlight, he found a body."

"A body?" Burt's eyes went wide in shock.

"A young man had been struck several times on the head with a tire wrench. Then he was dragged across the parking lot and thrown among the cactus to die."

"That's horrible."

"The dead man worked for Jack Ross. He delivered your car to the hotel last night." Reed referred to a page in his notebook. "It was around six-thirty or seven."

"Oh, my God...."

"I hate to bother you with all this, but he was driving your car. I thought you might have seen or heard something."

"No," Burt said struggling for control. "I heard nothing. I must have been giving my talk at that time in the banquet room."

"...And I was out by the pool on that other case." The D.E.A man flipped a page of his notebook. "In fact, we met out there, you were on your way to your room. Do you remember?"

"Very well."

"Do you know if your car had been returned before you went back to your room?"

"Yes, I think it was. In fact, I'm certain it was. Yes, I went into the car to get my keys and my receipt from the garage. They were left under the floor mat."

"And you didn't see anyone or hear anything. Like a car driving away?"

"No. Not a thing."

Cummins picked up his coffee cup, but put it back down without touching his lips. "I'm so sorry. That poor man. Why would anyone want to kill him?"

"In the dark the killer thought the driver was the rich owner of a very expensive automobile. Police believe the motive was robbery."

The D.E.A. man was lightly tapping his notebook with the stubby pencil. "I'm wondering if there might be some connection with that hubcap. Something somebody would kill for."

If Cummins had been hooked to a lie detector when the D.E.A man said 'hubcap,' he would have wrapped the needle around the peg.

"Hubcap?" Cummins choked.

"Your front hubcap was off." He closed the notebook. "Was it off when you went back to your room?"

"I returned through the patio doors."

"When you went out to get your garage receipt from under the floormat."

"I didn't notice. I must have gotten in on the right side."

"We found the hubcap in the parking lot. It is being checked for prints. We'll see you get it back."

"Thanks. Not that it matters, but that was a new hubcap."

"Yes, I know." Reed took a swallow of coffee and in midgulp he thought of a question to ask. "Do you have any idea as to what happened to the old one?"

"Not really." Cummins thought it was a good time to add a bit of truth to the conversation. Something that could be checked out. "I didn't know it was gone until a service station attendant brought it to my attention..." Cummins made an attempt to simulate a thoughtful countenance. "It was an all night 76 station." Cummins could see the needle spinning around the peg. Cold sweat was running down the inside of his arms as he anticipated the D.E.A. man's next question.

"Do you remember where that 76 station was?"

"Yes, I do. It was the all night 76 station in Yuma. I pulled in for gas and the attendant told me I was missing a hubcap. When I arrived here I looked up a Lincoln dealer in the phone book and had them put a new one on."

"Any special reason to buy one here rather than wait until you returned to Los Angeles?"

"No reason. Only a car looks...so shabby with a hubcap missing." Burt started to raise his coffee cup but put it down when he discovered his hand shaking. "I wish I had waited."

After a pause the D.E.A. man asked, "Isn't Yuma a great distance out of your way? Coming here from Los Angeles?"

The man's questions were building a fence around Cummins. Cummins' answers were adding the barbed wire.

"I guess I can tell you. It is really not as bad as it may sound." Cummins took a deep breath. "I stopped in San Diego to pick up a lady. She is here with me now. I'm sure I can trust your discretion."

"You just 'picked up' a girl in San Diego?"

"I told you it was not as bad as it may sound," Burt Cummins forcd a small laugh. "I've known this lady for some time. In fact, she is going to Los Angeles with me and she will be working in my office."

"Handy."

"It's not like that. Not at all. My wife and I have been separated for more than two years, even though we still share the same home."

"I'm sorry, I didn't mean..."

"No harm," Cummins took a quick sip of coffee. "I wish there was something I could do to help you but we must be in Los Angeles this afternoon, so I'll be leaving in a few minutes." Cummins was getting up out of his chair and reaching for his wallet.

"No, no. This is my treat," insisted Reed.

"Oh," Cummins laughed, "I wanted to give you my card. You can call me if there is anything else you want from me."

"That won't be necessary," Reed tapped his notebook. "I have it all here. I hope you don't mind. I got your address and phone number from the desk clerk, then verified it against your Master Card at the Jack Ross garage."

"You are way ahead of me," Cummins smiled, but as he looked down at the card he was about to give the D.E.A. man, his smile quickly fell apart. The card read MINI STORAGE - YOU KEEP THE KEY... This time he would have knocked the needle around the peg and the machine off the table.

The D.E.A. man was saying, "I can't help but feel that there is some connection between the fat guy in the pool last night and this killing." Reed was still flipping pages in search of a blank sheet when Cummins was half way up to his patio.

Reed watched Cummins until he saw him enter his room through the sliding doors. He then turned the notebook one more page. With the stub of his pencil, he wrote:

'In answer to question, "Did you notice the hubcap missing?" Suspect answered, "I didn't notice. I must have gotten in the right side." How did suspect know it was the left front hubcap that had been taken?'

The D.E.A. man closed his notebook and put it in his pocket and looked steadily at the patio drapes of room 2l2 as he finished his coffee.

Cummins entered his room and without a word to Mary, he hurried directly to the bathroom and took the Mini Storage card from his wallet, tore it into little pieces and flushed it down the toilet.

"Are you all right?" Mary called.

"No, I am not all right," he said coming from the bathroom, "I'm all wrong. Wrong. I damn near put both of us in jail...for murder."

"You what?"

"It's true. My big mouth. My bright ideas. My lies. I couldn't even tell the truth right. It was so close, I'm sick."

"What happened?" asked Mary.

"There's no time to explain. Throw everything in the car. I want to be away from here in two minutes. Don't try to pack, just throw."

Mary took her clothes from the closet and tossed them into the back seat of the Mark VI.

"What did you do with the wallet?" Cummins asked between trips to the car.

"I have it and I'll throw it from the car when we are on the road. The gun and the keys are in my purse."

"Good, let's go," urged Burt.

"Don't forget the briefcase under the bed."

"OH, SHIT."

They drove out of the hotel driveway only five seconds over the two minutes Cummins had allowed himself.

Before they had gone a block, and without looking at Mary, Cummins said, "Throw that Goddamn wallet out."

"Not yet," Mary answered. "There is a police car following right behind us."

"OH, SHIT."

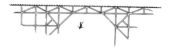

Reed walked through the hotel lobby exchanging morning greetings with other D.E.A. officers milling about, but he made no effort to encourage conversation. Instead, he returned only a smile and an acknowledging nod, and walked directly to the main desk. The man behind the counter turned as Reed came up.

"Good morning, may I help you?" asked the clerk.

Reed flipped open his wallet with a practiced move of his thumb to show his gold badge. The clerk gave a glancing look at the shield and said, "Yes, officer, what can I do for you?"

For all the examination the clerk gave the badge, it could have said, CHICKEN INSPECTOR. It always amazed Reed how completely people put their trust in a person who flashed a badge or wore a uniform. Dumb.

"Could I see the manager, please?"

"Is anything wrong? Perhaps I could help."

"No, I need some information. I wanted to go through the proper channels."

"The manager is out of town. Let me see if I can get the assistant manager." The clerk picked up his phone and pushed three numbers. After a short conversation, the man said, "If you will walk around the desk and down the hall you will find the assistant manager's office the third door on your left."

Reed followed the instructions and nearly tripped over a very large golf bag some tourist had left in his path. Down the hall he knocked lightly on the third door and a man's voice called, "Enter."

The door opened in and Reed saw the width of the door took almost half the room.

A young, middle-management type man with slick black hair and a thin mustache was seated at a desk not more than a foot deep. A letter lay on the top of the desk and left little margin at the top or bottom. Reed's expression must have shown his surprise, because the man said with a smile, "They took out two brooms and a mop and moved me in." The man rose from his chair. "I'm Jack Walsh, assistant manager, can I help you?"

"I'm Officer Reed," he flipped his badge. "You have HOBIC service in the hotel?"

"Yes, we do."

"I would like to see the teletype readout for room 212 for the past twelve hours."

Jack Walsh sat down behind his desk and motioned for Reed to have the only other chair in the room. When they were both seated, Walsh tapped a yellow pencil on the desk top as he considered the request.

"I guess that would be all right."

"It may be nothing. I'm quite sure it is, and the information could clear the subject."

"The HOBIC teletype is in the phone room next door. We can go there now if you like." Walsh rose from his chair and the two men jostled to find space to open the door and both get to the hallway.

The teletype paper came from the HOBIC printer onto a large takeup spool attached to the wall and the assistant manager began pulling the paper out by the yard, like wide toilet paper with sprocket holes along the edges.

"Did you say room 212?" Walsh asked without looking at Reed.

"Yes."

The assistant manager was now going hand over hand down the paper like a salesgirl measuring yard goods. "Here we are. Room 212. Buffer number is 44MS.. The MS stands for Mountain Shadows."

"Clever."

"Time 1400," Walsh looked up from the paper, "That is 2:00 AM."

"Yes, I know."

"Connection...three minutes...charges two dollars and thirty-five cents...area code 213, number called is 292-8827." The man gave a fast look at a few more feet of HOBIC printout paper. "That is all I can find for room 212. There may be others from yesterday...I'll look if you want."

Reed was writing in his notebook. "This is all I need. Thank you very much for your help."

"Always ready to lend a hand to the law." The man gave the official junior-executive corporate smile.

Reed put his notebook in his pocket and left the telephone room.

The assistant manager stood by the teletype machine knee deep in yards of paper. He turned to the switchboard operator and asked, "Who is in room 212?"

The operator checked her standing file, "Dr. Burton Cummins and wife...they checked out this morning."

"And...wife..." the assistant manager let the words hang. "I wonder whose."

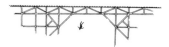

Reed had dialed the number on the lobby pay phone and the main office of the Arizona Department of Public Safety was putting his call through to his old friend, Capt. Robert Martin. Martin had joined the department when it was still called the Arizona State Police. He served through the Highway Patrol days and now, in his sixty-fifth year, he could say, except for two and a half years with the military police in Germany, a third of his life had been spent with the department. Now his main objective was to get nine more months behind him and retire.

"Captain Martin," he snapped into the phone while still thumbing through his recreation vehicle magazine.

"Vince Reed here, Captain." The D.E.A. man knew the reply he would receive.

"Hi. You old redhead son-of-a-bitch, how the hell are you? You caught me just in time. I'm gonna retire any minute now."

"They should have put you out to pasture years ago." They exchanged laughter. "Hey, Robert old buddy..."

"Oh, shit. When Vince Reed starts that 'Old Buddy' shit, it's time to count the silverware..." Martin laughed.

"I need a favor. Semi-official and all quiet."

"Name it."

Reed went on to give Captain Martin some background on the two homicides at the hotel and asked if he would check a name and address and all possible information from the Los Angeles telephone number.

"May take a few minutes. Do you want to hold on or can I call you?"

Reed gave him the number of the pay phone he was using and said he would wait for his call. He thanked the Captain and hung up.

To hold the phone for the expected call, he stood in front of it and kept turning pages in the directory. After stalling for fifteen minutes, he felt the need to relieve himself and he went into the nearby men's room.

When he returned, a short, middle-aged, heavy-set woman dressed in a loud, green and yellow Hawaiian MuMuu, was at his phone. The little lady strained to reach the coin slot and dial. The phone to her right was only four feet off the floor and the government had insisted the phone company and the hotel spend much extra money to install such units so short people and people in wheel chairs would have easy access to the dial and the slots. The lady had bypassed the special phone, installed just for her dimensions, and she strained and struggled with the standard height unit. It figures, thought Reed, the City pays thousands to install signal lights at busy intersecions and people still kill themselves crossing in the middle of the block. Dumb.

"Hello Sara," the little lady had the phone to her ear but was stretching her neck and yelling as if the mouthpiece were on the phone near the dial as was the style years back. "I'm calling about our get-together tonight. You and I and the lady who lives by you. Yes, I know. Well, I was wondering if maybe you might want to go to a movie show, or you might rather go the Windmill Theatre. Yea, eat and see a stage play. Cesar Romero is there this week... How should I know the name of the play? Who cares? I would just like to see Cesar Romero... He sure is... Yes, I remember. He was dancing with Carmen Miranda...CARMEN MIRANDA... With the fruit on the hat. Yeah... I Give to Cesar Romero the things that are Cesar's...or anything else he wants... Listen Sara, I got to tell you..."

Vince Reed gave a look at his wristwatch and saw he had been waiting over thirty minutes. Then a man walked up to use the phone on the left. Reed moved to the short phone and, bending his six foot frame, he dialed the Department of Safety.

"Hello, this is Officer Vince Reed again. I wanted to give Captain Martin another number where he..." he began to explain.

"Captain has been trying to reach you," said the operator, "but your line has been busy. Hold please and I'll connect you with Captain Martin's office."

Vince Reed was still bending over to the phone like a grown man drinking at a child's water fountain, and to make it more embarrassing, the man and the short lady had finished their conversations and had walked away, leaving him alone at the bank of phones.

"Vince. I got everything I could," Captain Martin began. "First, it is an unlisted number in Beverly Hills, big deal. Also an office phone listed to the same party. That number is 944-4420 and the address is 2424 Pearl, also in Beverly Hills. Name is Hendricks. J. M. Hendricks. The company is Hendricks and Cooper. The partner, Ralph Cooper, was killed about two and a half years ago. Foul play was evident. Nothing was ever proven and no arrests were made. Cooper's widow is still employed with the company. The rundown on that operation is that it is a schlocky talent agency and audition service. Company has not been franchised by any of the Holywood guilds. This guy Hendricks has been mixed up in some southpaw political movements and his company is now under investigation for false and misleading advertising and using the mails to defraud. There may be more on the wire later," Martin concluded.

"Thanks, Robert. This will do," Reed was saying as he scribbled the last line in his notebook. "That was fast work."

"We've been computerized," the Captain said. "You could have had it sooner, but your phone was busy." He had his laugh.

"So long Captain, and thanks," Reed put the phone back on the hook and straightened up and moved to a normal height phone and made one more call.

"Good morning, Western Airlines, Nancy speaking."

"Good morning. What is the next flight I can get to Los Angeles?"

Interstate 10, west of Blyth, California, climbs a steep grade to one hundred and seventy-five feet above the valley floor in less than eight miles. Before you are half-way to the summit, your rear-view mirror reflects acres of green fields of alfalfa and sudan hay, all sectioned off in quarter mile grids by white concrete canals and irrigation berms. The water, drawn from the Colorado River, flows along these ditches, keeping the crops of the Palo Verde Valley growing green year round. A drastic contrast to the high, rolling sand dunes of the unirrigated, barren lands that fall away to the south.

After the highway levels off at the apex of the hill, and you lose the view of the fertile fields, you enter, what is known as, Chuckawalla Flats, named for the dark colored desert lizard, the only denizen of this high mesa that stretches an uninterrupted one hundred miles of squat greasewood scrub and jojoba bush. The far, monotonous horizon is broken only by an occasional dust devil, a waltzing serpentine pillar of red desert top soil, swirling into powerful whirlwinds hundreds of feet into the sky, then to suddenly vanish, only to reappear as a ghostly eddy on another part of the desert floor where the mad pirouttes continue with new partners.

By the time the Mark VI had passed Desert Center, Mary had finished explaining to Burt why she had gone back to their hotel room to change clothes. How, in desperation during her struggle, her hand found the banderillas and how she had driven them into the back of the fat man.

Remembering the lab report the D.E.A. man had told him about on the man in the pool, Burt asked, "He didn't do anything to you, did he?"

"He almost twisted my arms off, he slapped my face raw and choked me till I nearly passed out."

"You didn't 'pass-out,' did you?" Burt continued the interrogation.

"No, I didn't pass out."

"Then he didn't...rape you." His question was a statement.

"Of course not."

"He did nothing...sexually to you?"

"Hell, no." Mary's temper was fast coming to a boil.

'That's not a very nice way to..."

"I just wanted the whole picture," Burt cut in. "You don't have to get angry."

"Well, I am angry and I'm angry because I'm scared. I'm scared to death." Suddenly Mary was crying. "In the past twelve hours three men have died and I murdered two of them."

"Who said anything about murder for God's sake?"

"You did. In the room, after talking with that policeman, you said...Murder." Mary's eyes were wet, tears were running down her cheek and dripping from here chin.

"Mary, that fat guy tried to kill you, you struck him in self defense and he fell into the pool and drowned. You didn't kill him and you certainly didn't murder him. No way. Strictly self defense."

"And the guy I hit with the brick," Mary was sobbing. "Was that self defense?"

"He was within a half second of killing me. If you hadn't hit him I would be dead now. Don't you understand?"

"I understand and you understand, but with a car full of coke and a killer's gun in my purse and three bodies back there...I don't think anyone else is going to."

"I admit it will take some explaining."

"You can bet your buns it will take a hell of a lot of explaining." Mary was crying again. "I'm not sure we can."

"O.K. I'll throw away the coke. I'll toss the gun out the window, whatever you want, you say it and I'll do it. Just don't let yourself fall apart. You did not murder anyone. You didn't evn commit manslaughter. You saved your own life and you sure as hell saved mine."

Mary drew five sheets of Kleenex from the chrome dispenser under the dash, bunched them on one hand and pressed them to her nose. "We don't have much choice, do we?" she said after gaining some control. "You can't throw the coke away because you'll need it to bargain for your wife. You might need the gun, too,'' her sobs were buried in the wet tissues.

''Mary, please.'' Burt tried to comfort her. ''I'll figure some way out of this. The tough part is all behind us.''

Mary was crying audibly and the combination of guilt and fright she had kept so tightly pent up came gushing in release.

Burt had told Mary, 'the tough part was behind them,' but he knew what was ahead this day would be the real danger.

Burt Cummins guided the Mark VI down the long, winding highway into the town of Indio. From Indio it would be less than three hours and they would be in Beverly Hills and as the miles passed, his apprehension grew. Burt was afraid of what unknown trouble lay ahead and he admitted it. The danger to himself he thought he could handle. The fear for the safety of his wife, frightening, but he was sure he could control the fear. He would be capable of any action to insure her safe return... Then into his mind, like the slow, tantalizing dance of the red dust devils back on Chuckwalla Flats, the most frightening thing of all. Burt Cummins was falling in love with the wonderful, beautiful young lady who sat beside him...and of this he was most frightened...and most ashamed.

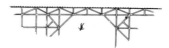

The seven man paramedic crew put their gear back in the bright red emergency truck and headed for Fire Station 17 to finish breakfast. There was nothing more they could do here, the man was dead.

Three white and black Phoenix police cars and an unmarked detective's car were crowded into the alleyway of the Camelback Mini Storage Warehouse. Two local television-news cars, their call letters and channel numbers garishly blazoned on the doors, were parked a short distance from the entrance. The reporters were tethered by microphone cable to the cameramen who carried their videotape cameras on their shoulders and the recorder power-pack slung at their sides. While the reporters took notes, the cameras were recording several shots of the body on the ground and action shots of the forensic team conducting their investigation.

One of the television reporters had gotten Lt. Tom Glen, a detective out of homicide, to stand in the alley so the camera could shoot him and have police action seen in the background. The Channel 10 reporter had asked a list of questions, but all the detective could tell him was that they had found a male caucasian, approximately forty years old, no identification, the pockets were empty and the wallet was missing, but an expensive watch and diamond ring had not been taken. The victim was wearing a shoulder holster, .38 short, and the holster was empty. As to the cause of death, the man apparently died from a blow to the back of the head. No weapon had been found, but the killer could have used a club or pipe or large rock. The reporter asked if the man might have been killed at another location and brought here and the detective said they believed the victim was killed at the Mini Warehouse. No motive was suggested and robbery was ruled out because of the watch and the diamond ring. The wallet may have been taken to throw the police off. The theory they were considering was that a narc buy could have run into a ripoff situation.

"One thing we did find should prove to be something," detective Glen said, as the cameras zoomed in for a close-up, "A clear set of thumb and palm prints on the heels of the victim's shoes."

"On his shoes?" questioned a reporter?

"It seems someone took a heel in each hand and pulled the body into the stall. The wax on the shoes held a perfect print."

"And you believe the prints are the prints of the murderer," a reporter offered.

"It will put someone here at the scene of the crime, if the prints aren't those of the dead man. You know...when he put his shoes on. The lab should have some answers in a few hours."

Before Detective Glen went back to the investigation, he told the reporters that the manager of the Mini Storage had placed the original call to the police. He then pointed to the manager.

Cameras and reporters quickly circled the manager. A reporter got a cue from his cameraman that the tape was rolling, and he asked:

"At what time did you find the body?"

"I was walking down between the buildings, like I do every morning, picking up trash and papers and things. I saw something on the ground. It was coming from under the door of stall 207 and it looked like blood. I went right away and called the police."

A second reporter asked the manager, "Do you know who the dead man is?"

"The police might know, they didn't tell me and I don't really care to know. Only, he ain't the man who rented 207."

The cameras zoomed in again.

"Who did rent the stall?" an off-screen voice asked.

"I don't have his name actually. I already told the police. The man who rented the stall said he had a new company coming to Phoenix and he needed storage for files and boxes and that sort of thing."

"Did he give a name?" the CBS man asked.

"Only said his company was Vantage...or something like that."

"Just Vantage? No other name?"

"Did he pay by check?" asked another.

"No. Paid cash," answered the manager.

The fourth television newsman to arrive carried his own camera and asked his questions while squinting into the viewfinder.

"Was there anyone with the man who rented the space?"

"I didn't see no one. The man was driving a big white car. Cadillac or Lincoln. What I do know is that the lock on the door was not the lock I sold him. I sold him an American combination lock and when we went to open the door it was a Master combination. Fire Department had to cut if off."

A reporter asked, "Did you hear anything. Like an argument or fight?"

"No, sir. I didn't hear nothing. I sleep at the back of that building with my window open and I can hear a cat walking through this place," the manager boasted. "No, I didn't hear nothing."

A reporter said, "Thank you, Mr...?"

"Jefferies, Samuel Jefferies," then, "What time will this be on?"

"Six o'clock, and thank you, Mr. Jefferies, you have been most helpful," and the crews hurried back to their stations.

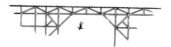

The 20 by 20 cell, in which Mrs. Martha Cummins had been confined for the past ten hours, would more aptly be called a cage. She sat on a low, canvas army cot. To her back was the dirty cement wall of the basement under the Hendricks & Cooper building. Facing her, and on each side, were walls of heavy gauge cyclone fencing from floor to ceiling. The center section having a narrow wire door held secure with lock and chain. A flickering fluorescent tube in a rusting fixture hung from a beam in the ceiling. On a wooden packing case, pressed into service as a table, stood a tall green wine bottle filled with water. In the corner, to her right, was a toilet. No door or partition, just a toilet attached to the wall. There was no seat and no cover and no paper. Heavy brown rust stains colored the bowl, inside and out.

Mrs. Cummins had not seen her 'cage.' She had been blindfolded since she was taken from her home the morning before.

Two of Hendricks' men had come to her front door. They were dressed as city utility workers. While one man asked questions as to the number of electrical appliances she had in her kitchen, the second man flung an arm around her head and placed an ether soaked rag over her nose and mouth. Her limp body was carried to a waiting van and brought to the office of Hendricks & Cooper. When she came out of the anesthetic, she found herself blindfolded and her wrists taped together.

After a short time in the upper office, which included the telephone call to her husband in Phoenix, Mrs. Cummins was brought down the elevator and put in the cage.

Martha Cummins had lost all track of time and she sat on the cot crying until she lowered her head to the gritty canvas and fell asleep. Her feet still on the floor.

The sun was burning off the last of the morning fog that, at daybreak this time of year, drifts in off the Pacific in gauzey whisps and floats silently through Beverly Hills, coating streets, cars and buildings with a fine oily mist, as if the entire town had been atomized with Vaseline.

At 9:00 AM, Hendricks swung his black Mercedes, with the patent leather shine, into the parking lot behind the Hendicks & Cooper building. He brought the car to an abrupt stop with both front wheels pressing hard against the cement curbing, where the word PRIVATE was painted in bold, red letters on a solid white background. He hurriedly climbed the outside, iron staircase at the rear of the building, pressed the oversized doorbell and looked directly into the closed-circuit television camera mounted over the door. A loud buzz was heard and Hendricks opened the door and entered.

Passing his secretary's desk the surprised lady looked up. "Good morning, Mr. Hendricks." She gave a quick look at the combination clock/calendar on the corner of her desk. It was 9:02. Hendricks was at least one hour early for his normal punctual arrival. This being Tuesday, his morning for raquet ball at the health club, he was four hours early.

"Have Phillips get the Cummins woman some coffee, then bring her to my office..." Hendricks kept walking, "...and leave the blindfold on."

"Jim." The secretary's voice stopped Hendricks but he did not turn to face her.

"Jim, please..." the lady rose to her feet and leaned across the desk, resting her weight on her two hands. "I can't take it any more...you promised... It has been more than a week now...please you must help me...you must."

Hendricks turned and spoke to the woman with complete irritation in his voice and manner. "Mrs. Cooper...you will remember your place, and you will also remember that this is an office, my office." Hendricks advanced two strides toward her. "Your personal problems and needs will not be discussed here...now or ever. If you have not yet learned to budget your supply...your lack of self control can hardly be blamed on me, now, can it?" Hendricks moved very close to the desk and the woman sank slowly to her chair. "You have friends...you've gone to them before...go to them, see if they will help you. See if they will help you as I have helped you...See if they will do what I have done for you..."

"I have told you many times how grateful I am to you for helping me after Paul died..." Mrs. Cooper did not look up but kept her head bowed. "I have told you and I have shown you."

"Mrs. Cooper, I do not expect gratitude, not even a thank you..." Hendricks leaned over the desk and his voice threatened, "Anything you ever did for me was more for your own gratification and desire. Paul Cooper never found out that the woman he married was a tramp... I helped you keep that secret from him...and you paid for that help... Well, Paul is gone now. There is no need to protect that spineless worm's ego any more. You were a tramp, you are a tramp, and you will never be anything but a two-bit tramp." The joy felt by Hendricks for this harangue was evident as his disdainful smile dissolved into a sneer. "There is nothing more disgusting than a fifty year old ex-hooker that has acquired a habit that her body can no longer pay for. Now, you can sit there and do your job, little as it is, or you can get your ass out of my building..." Hendricks drew himself to his most righteous full height. "Have I made myself perfectly clear?"

Mrs. Cooper did not answer, as she had not answered to the many such tirades she had been forced to endure over the past years. Her only response was a small nod of understanding.

"Now enough of this...There is work to be done and if you can't do it, I will find someone who can. Get Phillips and do as I told you." Hendricks turned and walked into his office and went directly to the telephone and pressed the intercom button.

"Yes, Mr. Hendricks." Mrs. Cooper answered in a haulting voice.

"Go to our master file and check for a Dr. Burton Cummins. Anything at all. Cross check our lit of psychiatrists in the Los Angeles area who are known users. If possible, a list of Dr. Cummins' patients and if any of them are known users." There was not a trace of the venom that had so filled his speech only moments before. "Also contact 'Lady Snow' and every 'head shop' in town. Get on this right away."

"Yes, Mr. Hendricks." Once again Mrs. Helen Cooper had been put in her place.

Hendricks replaced the phone, moved behind his desk and sat down. The palms of his hands rubbing small circles on the polished wooden arms of his leather chair. He could easily put Mrs. Cooper out of his mind. She would not be a bother again for quite some time... His concern now was for Robert Johnson, and his two million dollar shipment of cocaine.

"Heavy connections," he was saying over and over. "What 'heavy connections'?" Hendricks rose from his chair and began pacing his office. He paused evry time around to look out the floor-to-ceiling windows to watch the morning trafic crawling, stop-and-go, up the avenue...his frustration building as he noted the number of cars pulling into the parking lot of his pseudo talent agency one floor blow, knowing that every fifth car was here to pick up their special cassette order...and his supply was running low... If he were to run out, his hard to collect clientele of writers, producers, directors and actors would look for another source. He did not want to risk losing the important influence he now enjoyed over these people and their lives and the content of their particular endeavors and he listed the crafts in the order of their importance.

"If Johnson is trying to double cross me... If this eight hour gag is a stall... A stall giving him time to contact my clients..." Hendricks was again thinking aloud. "If it is a double cross, I'll know how to handle it. I took care of it when Cooper tried to take over...I can do it again."

Hendricks continued to look to the broad avenue, still no black Datsun with Arizona plates was to be seen.

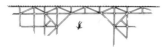

The noisy rattle of the elevator woke Mrs. Cummins with a start. She was still in darkness and it took a full minute for her to rise to a sitting position. She heard the clanking of the lock and chain and the squeek of the door when Miss Phillips entered her cage. The husky voice said, ''They want to talk to you up-stairs. Here's some coffee.'' The matron of a woman, put the styrofoam cup on the wooden box.

From her darkness Mrs. Cummins asked, ''Would it be too much trouble to get me a Bloody-Mary?''

''Way too much.'' Miss Phillips was abrupt and sarcastic.

''But it's cold and wet in here.'' Mrs. Cummins complained.

''Drink your coffee, go to the toilet and be ready to go upstairs. I'll be back in five minutes.''

Miss Phillips went out the door, locking it behind her with some extra slamming and clanking to give the desired effect.

Mrs. Cummins waited until she heard the elevator start. She moved her bound hands over the wooden box at the end of her cot and her fingers touched the neck of the wine bottle. Then she lowered her hands and felt the edge of the cup and the steam from the coffee. Carefully she raised the cup to her mouth... Black coffee. How she hated black coffee... She took a sip and placed the cup back on the box... With great effort she rose to her feet and moved, at a shufle, along the wall to her right. Her leg bumped the cold porcelain of the toilet bowl.

The indignity of it, thought Mrs. Cummins, as she worked her clothes as best she could with her bound wrists. "The idea of treating a person this way... and for no reason." She had no way of knowing if she had privacy or if that woman was still there watching. Mrs. Cummins had not seen Miss Phillips. She was judging only from her voice. A voice that had a tinge and tonal quality of a central European nation. And whatever nation it was, she must have been a matron in a woman's prison...or a man's prison...or Devil's Island...Martha Cummins' imagination pictured Miss Phillips as heavy and tall, straw-blond hair with a bun at the back of her head. Tight, milkey white skin drawn over prominent cheek bones and forehead. Her dress would be plain and it would come half way down below her knees ...black knit socks and brown shoes with flat heels...Wagner's 'Brunnehilde.' If Martha could have seen Miss Phillips, she would have been amazed how closely her imagined description fit the woman.

Mrs. Cummins fumbled with the handle and managed to flush the toilet. She adjusted her clothes...moved to what what she thought was the center of the room...and waited.

When the noise of the elevator was heard again, it seemed to be behind her and she turned. The sound of the door being unlocked was now in front of her.

"Back up, damn it. Back up." Phillips was yelling as the steel door brushed Mrs. Cummins off balance. "Come on you, they want you in the office."

Miss Phillips took hold of Martha's arm and led her out of the cage and onto the small elevator.

One element in her imagined description of Miss Phillips had been overlooked. Her breath. Now, in the confines of the elevator, her picture was completed.

After fifteen minutes of pacing, Hendricks jerked the phone from its cradle and pressed the buzzer.

"Yes, Mr. Hendricks?"

"What is keeping that Cummins woman?"

"Miss Phillips is coming out of the elevator now."

Within seconds Miss Phillips opened the door to Hendricks' private office and sternly led Mrs. Cummins in by the arm. An over-conscientious school teacher presenting an unmanageable student to the principal.

"Sit down, Mrs. Cummins," said Hendricks.

As Hendricks' voice came to her out of the blackness, Martha Cummins stood confused and frightened, like the newly blind, not knowing if a chair was behind her. For a moment she made no move, then she felt the leading edge of the chair pressed firmly against the back of her knees and the strong hand of Miss. Phillips on her shoulder forcing her down onto the chair.

Hendricks made a motion of dismissal and Miss Phillips left the office, closisng the door behind her.

"I trust you were not too uncomfortable, Mrs. Cummins." Hendricks' mock concern went unheard, as Martha Cummins began to speak:

"Why are you people holding me here? What do you want from me? What have you done to my husband? What has happened to him?" Her voice was more demanding than pleading.

"Nothing has happened to your husband," Hendricks said, believing he was lying. "But unless you give me the information I want...something might happen to him...like getting himself killed."

Martha Cummins fought back tears. She had never cowed to anyone, and she wasn't about to now...if she could help it. "I don't know what you are talking about," she insisted.

Hendricks moved from his chair to the front of his desk and sat on the corner, looking down on Martha Cummins.

"To put it bluntly, Mrs. Cummins... I know your husband has connections with the sale of...drugs." He let the word fall heavy.

"Drugs?" Mrs. Cummins answered in surprise. Then, after a beat, "Oh, drugs...sale of drugs... Yes, yes, he does... How did you find that out?" she demanded.

"Never mind how I found out..." Hendricks could hardly contain himself.

"That is a personal matter between Burt and my brother. Whatever would you want with that?"

"Mrs. Cummins," Hendricks spoke deliberately. "I don't have much time, so listen very closely... Does your husband have access to drugs from your brother?"

"Yes, but no one was supposed to know anything about that," Mrs. Cummins clasped her fingers together and beat them on her knees. "Burt is going to be furious when he hears of this... It has to do with permits or taxes...or something."

"Mrs. Cummins, do you know what kind of drugs your husband has been getting from your brother?"

"How would I know that? All I know is that George, my brother, sends a box every month or so..."

"Where does he send this box?"

"To our home... Now, please may I go? I've told you everything you wanted to know."

"Not quite," Hendricks said as he moved back to his chair and picked up a pen. "I need your brother's address."

Mrs. Cummins thought for a moment. "I did know their address... Let me think...I had a Christmas card from them and I sent one to them... Oh dear... You've made me so nervous I can't remember."

"Take your time. Think... It's very important... The address."
Hendricks had his pen poised above his note pad.

"His name is George B. Thompson..." Martha Cummins didn't
want to give any information...yet she was afraid not to and more
afraid of what would happen if she gave him false information. "You
could look him up in the phone book."

Hendricks was writing on the pad, "George B. Thompson."

"The company name is Rocky Mountain Wholesale Pharmaceutical
Supply."

Hendricks' mind went racing. The chance to obtain the real thing.
Pharmaceutical coke. His distribution would more than double. Writers, producers, network brass, he'd have little trouble convincing them
to flavor their scripts as he directed. This was the pry, the fulcrum he
needed. All that remained was to make this connection.

"The company is in Las Vegas..." Mrs. Cummins began.

"Vegas?" Hendricks almost shouted.

Mrs. Cummins was about to give the address and zip number, but
before she could get the first number out of her mouth, Hendricks was
talking and pushing his intercom button.

"That will be all, Mrs. Cummins."

"Will you let me go home now? I won't say anything to anyone.
Just let me go home...please." Mrs. Cummins was crying now.

Into the phone Hendricks ordered Miss Phillips to return their hostage to the basement and have his secretary contact his people in
Vegas.

After Miss Phillips had taken Mrs. Cummins out of the office,
Hendricks sat at his desk rubbing his hands together.

"How the hell did that shithead Johnson find out about this?"
Hendricks was asking himself. "Did he luck out and overhear something, or did he force the information out of the doctor before he killed
him?" Then a sobering thought struck. "If that son-of-a-bitch is on his
way to Vegas... If that is what the eight hour sham was for..." Hendricks rose from his chair again. "If he thinks he can move in... But he
wouldn't have tipped me to this information if he were going to try
something." Hendricks walked to the window again. "Where the hell
is he?"

Going back to his desk he pressed the intercom button.

"Yes, Mr. Hendricks."

"What the hell is taking so long for that Vegas call?"

"I'm still trying, Mr. Hendricks... Pamela Cook is holding on line three...can you talk to her now?" his secretary asked.

"Tell her I'll get back to her as soon as I can."

"She said it is very important."

"I'll decide what's important...you tell her that," and he slammed the phone down.

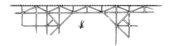

It was 3:05, Pacific Standard Time. The Mark VI cut from the Hollywood Freeway onto the Wilshire offramp. Burt Cummins had driven the four hundred and twenty-five miles in slightly over eight hours. A stop for gas and coffee had taken only eleven minutes in Banning.

Cummins drove into a large 76 station and stopped in front of a bank of telephone booths. Finding no dimes in his pockets, he put a quarter in the slot and dialed his home. There were several rings before the maid answered:

"Cummins' residence," the maid said with caution in her voice.

"Corla, it's me, Dr. Cummins."

"Oh, Doctor... I have been trying to reach you all day..." The maid was in tears and on the brink of hystria. "Mrs. Cummins... I can't find her anywhere...I've called and called...I went to the store and did a few errands...when I returned Mrs. Cummins was gone...her car was here but she was gone."

"I know, Corla... I know..."

"I called the police. They said to wait till tomorrow and I should call them again if Mrs. Cummins was still missing. They said 'missing'."

"Corla... Now listen... Mrs. Cummins is safe... I talked with her... I can't explain now but I want you to pack a few things and take the car and go to a hotel... My Gulf card is in the Olds...in the glove compartment. Take it and go to the Holiday Inn on Sunset...right by the Freeway...I'll call as soon as I can."

"What is happening?" the maid pleaded. "I'm worried sick... Mrs. Cummins didn't act like anything was wrong...just asked me to get some things from the store...like usual, now she's gone." Corla began to cry.

Cummins tried to reassure her. "Please Corla... Do like I say...right now...take the car and go to the Holiday Inn and stay there until I call or come by for you."

Corla hung up the phone. Burt waited a long time trying to gather his thoughts. He was casting about, looking at nothing in particular when he caught sight of the sign. A forty foot billboard high overhead. The scene was a golden sunset at the beach. A young man and a young woman walking hand in hand...barefoot in the wet sand... Across the top of the sign, 'When you want good taste, and low tar...' At a slight angle was a floating package of VANTAGE cigarettes... The pack was eighteen feet tall and three of the cigarettes were sticking out of the pack above the billboard... Vantage. The sight sent a chill through his body. The last pack he had seen was in that glass ashtray... The Mini Storage... Space 207... A man lying dead on the floor...his head bashed in...blood... "What name?" the funny looking man with the bushy eyebrows had asked. "Vantage" Burt had answered... Burt walked back to the car.

"Well?" asked Mary. "What did you find out?"

Burt was still looking at the giant billboard. "See that pack of cigarettes?" he asked.

"Yes, I see it."

"That pack of Vantage... That pack of Vantage has a Goddamn 'BULLS-EYE' on it."

Mary studied Burt's face. "I don't know what the hell you are talking about... Did you call home?"

"Yes, yes... I called home," his voice suddenly irate.

Mary waited for more.

"Give me that business card for Hendricks and Cooper."

"All I have are the keys and the gun... You told me to tear up all those cards and flush them down the toilet..."

"Damn it, I didn't mean that card, too." Burt was still looking at the 'Bull's Eye.' "How will I find the address now?"

Without an answer, Mary opened her door and went dirctly to the booth Cummins had just come out of. She picked up the white pages and leafed through to the H's... Her eyes followed a slightly painted fingernail down the column. When she found Hendricks & Cooper, she ripped the page from the book and returned to the car. Once inside, she read the address. "Hendricks & Cooper, 2424 Pearl..."

"Where is Pearl?" Burt asked all bland.

"How the hell should I know?"

Mary angrily climbed out of the car again and walked to the office of the gas station. Four young attendants were more than willing to tell her where Pearl Street was, and the easiest way to get there. One offerd to take her there.

Getting back in the car, Mary said flatly, "Eleven blocks ahead and to the right." She sat up very straight, her arms crossed defiantly.

Burt Cummins made no answer, put the car in gear and moved into the west bound Wilshire traffic. The four young, goodlooking attendants stood in line as the car passed in review. They all waved 'bye-bye,' one clutched his heart and swooned into the arms of his buddy... the fourth held a length of water hose in an obscene manner and sang, 'Be My Love.' Mary sneaked a look and a smile... Burt Cummins was looking straight ahead.

Mary was silently counting the blocks. "Two more blocks, then right," she finally said.

"I know, I know."

"Burt, I'm only trying to help, for God's sake."

"I'm sorry, Mary. I'm sorry... We are almost there and I don't know what in the hell I am going to do... I just don't know."

"Why not pull over and park while we work out a plan?"

Burt pulled into the first available space...there was still one block to go.

Mary was watching people who crowded the sidewalk, the cars moving past in a continuous parade.

"Let's leave the car and walk." Mary suggested. "Look the place over...see what they have."

"It can't hurt." Burt stepped out on the traffic side and moved around to open Mary's door. "What do they say in the movies... We'll case the joint?"

"Something like that." Mary gave an 'all's forgiven' smile. "Don't forget the briefcase."

Burt reached back into the car for the briefcase, and they walked side by side up Wilshire. At the corner, they turned right...halfway up the block they saw it... The two story building...Hendricks & Cooper. The front had narrow windows from street level to the top of the building...the sides were solid brick...no windows.

Burt stopped. He slowly shook his head from side to side. "I can't believe Martha is somewhere in that building. I don't feel anything. Wouldn't you think I would have some feeling... being this close...some vibration...something...if she was in there? Shouldn't I feel some force to make me want to run into that building...shouldn't I feel something?"

Mary walked beside Cummins as they neared the entrance, then she turned to face him. "How about some spaghetti?"

"Spaghetti?" Burt could not believe she had said that... "How can you even think of food now?"

"I'm not thinking of food, but we should be able to get some information from that Italian restaurant next door. They might know something about their neighbor."

Burt had to let that all sink in for a moment. His mind was not too receptive and sorting took time. "Sure, that makes sense." They fell in step and walked past the front of the Hendricks & Cooper Building with only a slight glance at the front windows. All they saw was an oscillating reflection of themselves...he with a briefcase with three plastic bags of coke on the inside...she with keys and a snubnose .38 in her purse.

The manager escorted them to a small table halfway to the back of the restaurant. A red and white checkered tablecloth, four bentwood chairs, bread sticks standing in a tall glass at the center of the table. Next to that, a sugar shaker with the top covered with pencil sized holes and filled with golden Romano cheese. The aroma of garlic and olive oil drifting from the kitchen. Overhead, hundreds of empty Chianti bottles in their straw wrappings, hanging from latticework below the imitation leaves and large bunches of plastic grapes.

The menue was a cardboard cut-out of a gondola. The waiter was dressed as the typical Venetian Gondolier and he came up to their table singing a theme from Rigoletto. He finished with a wide 'Pavarotti' smile, if not the voice.

"You like'a dat a'song?" the waiter asked while whisking away some imaginary crumbs with a napkin. "Dat'a song was written by a countryman of mine... Joe Green." He was doing his Dom DeLuise schtick, but a hundred pounds lighter. "You see...I can make'a fun of Joe Green, or if you prefer, Giuseppe Verde, because'a he himself said those immortal words, 'Tutto mondo e burla,' or if you can't read the Italian side of the menu, 'All the World's a Joke,' ha, ha, ha."

Then with sudden seriousness he held his pencil over his order pad, "What you a'gonna have?"

Mary gave a little laugh and that was all the waiter needed to bolster his confidence, a receptive audience, no matter how small.

"If I had gotten laughs like that at the Comedy Store, I wouldn't be here slinging spa'get."

"You are an actor?" Cummins asked while reading the menu.

"I thought I was a stand-up comic. Gags, impressions, big ending with a song." The waiter held out his arms in a Taa-Daa finish.

"So?" asked Mary, still with a giggle.

"I didn't get any laughs with my gags so... I never got to do my big finish."

"That's a shame." Mary's tone was serious and caring.

"Why, thank you maam," the waiter went into his Walter Brennen, which wasn't easy wearing a Gondolier's wide brim straw hat with a long red ribbon hanging down his back. "I just bet you be an actress yourself...or 'dad-ratted, you should be...you're pretty...yes, maam...you're about the best all'over goodlookin woman I ever see..."

Burt looked at Mary then at the waiter. "Matter of fact, that is why we are here in Hollywood...to see if I can find something for her in telvision...commercials, maybe."

The waiter's eyes never left Mary's face... "Very, very possible... Very possible. You even look like a movie star. I can't remember the name, she was in a picture with Glenn Ford, you sure look like her. You'd be great in television."

"I was thinking about this talent agent next door. Do you know anything about them?" Burt probed.

The waiter looked in both directions to be sure no one could hear. Bending over the table, he said, "I don't know of one person who ever got a job through them...not one." The waiter gave another quick look, then leaned even closer. "Mike, the young guy we have parking cars, he finally got a job on CHIPS...only three days, but it is a network show. You know how he got the job? The producer was eating here, saw him and gave him the job. Mike had been with that bunch next door for over a year and they never even sent him out on a 'cattle call'."

"Cattle call?" asked Mary.

"Yeah. Sometimes a picture needs a lot of people and the agents send everyone they got to show up for an audition. That is a 'cattle call'...I don't know how these yo-yo's stay in business, but they do... Parking lot is always filled. Poor Mike. He spent a ton on money on pictures, tapes, acting lessons. They gave him the full treatment... They've done it to hundreds, I'll bet.''

"Then they make money." said Cummins.

"Like a pay toilet in a diarrhea ward,'' the waiter quipped. "No...a pretty thing like you should go to MCA, or William Morris, or Tobias...somebody like that. There are hundreds of good agents in this town...don't get mixed up with these schlocks.''

Cummins put his menu on the table and moved his chair back. "I don't think we will have time to eat right now...we'll be back." Burt reached in his wallet and drew out a five dollar bill and put it on the menu. "Thanks for the information.''

The waiter stepped back and gave a frightened look to the manager, who was standing behind the cash register. People leaving without ordering...the look from the manager was enough to send the waiter packing.

"I'm sorry you can't stay...'' the waiter stammered.

"It's my fault. I forgot how late it was. We'll be back, I promise.'' Cummins assisted Mary from her chair and they started for the door... Mary turned to Burt:

"You'll have to wait a minute while I go to the ladies' room.'' Mary headed for the door marked 'FEMINA.'

"I'll call my office.'' Burt said to her back. "I should have done it before now.'' He moved to the wall phone at the far end of the counter, near the door.

As Cummins dialed the number, he could hear the restaurant manager yelling at their waiter:

"You talk'a too damn a'much...you got all ah'da time with your God 'a' damn mouth...you don't a'give nobody da'time to eat.'' The manager was not doing his Dom DeLouise, he was doing his Firing A Waiter schtick.

While Cummins waited for his office phone to answer, he remembered from his studies how very much the 'no-talents' of the world seemed to relish the opportunity of pushing, belittling and openly insulting a person of 'talent.' An act even more vocal and savoring to them when performed before an audience... The 'no-talent' is in fact more of a 'ham' than the 'talent.'

Like the kids of old, throwing a snowball at the man with the top hat...or throwing the rock through the window of the 'rich kid's' home...this waiter was saddled with that type of mental dwarf.

180

"Dr. Cummins' office." His secretary's voice was firm and normal.

"Joan... This is Dr. Cummins. I wanted to..."

"Dr. Cummins," Joan cut in, her voice now all but falling apart. "Doctor, there have been police all over the place... Your maid called several times...said she couldn't find Mrs. Cummins...now the police are here...I've been so worrid."

"The police are there...now?" Burt asked in surprise.

"Two in your office and one waiting in the hall."

"Are they asking about Mrs. Cummins?" Burt's words were tiptoeing along.

"No... something about Phoenix... What's wrong Doctor?"

Burt was hit between the eyes with another baseball bat.

"Joan, listen... Don't say anything about this call. I'll get back to you as soon as I can... Don't worry... There is nothing to worry about."

Cummins hung up the phone. A white-hot poker lay in his chest. Dread and complete helplessness filled his entire body. His mouth dry, his breathing forced in gulps. Perspiration was standing out on his forehead and running freely down his suddenly pale cheeks, like a man struck with fever.

As Mary returned to the front of the restaurant, she saw Burt's condition and rushed the last few feet up to him.

"Burt, what happened? What's wrong?"

"Get me outside, hurry please."

Cummins could hardly walk. The manager had followed his waiter into the kitchen and Mary was alone to assist Burt through the door.

Once on the street, Mary asked again, "Burt, what is it? What has happened to you?"

Cummins was still clawing for breath. "Police. The police are waiting at my office."

"Police? Oh, Burt. Is it something about your wife? My God. Has anything happened to your wife?"

With more control Burt said, "The police are from Phoenix."

"Phoenix?"

"Not from Phoenix... They are here...because of Phoenix."

"What are we going to do?" Mary put the fingers of both her hands over her mouth.

"I don't know, I don't know."

They started walking toward the corner when Mary stopped short. "BURT...LOOK."

There, not fifty yards ahead of them, parked in the street beside their Mark VI, was a black-and-white police car and two policemen standing next to it on the sidewalk.

Shielded from the view of the police by the throng of passing pedestrians, Burt grabbed Mary's arm and wrenched her in the opposite direction and hurried back to the entrance of Hendricks & Cooper and through the glass doors.

Still unsteady, and wiping the sweat from his face with a handkerchief, Burt approached the receptionist seated behind the low horseshoe desk. The blond looked up from her magazine. "Is there something I can do for you?" she smiled.

Burt was doing a Louis Armstrong with the handkerchief in his right hand and holding the briefcase across his chest with his left:

"Hello... I'd like to see someone...about commercials. Television..." and as an afterthought, turning to indicate Mary, "For her."

"Yes, sir," the blond said as she brought out a legal size sheet of paper with printing on each side. "If you will fill out this form please."

Burt took the paper from the girl and said, "Is this necessary? I don't have much time."

"I'm sorry, but we need this information... It won't take long... Really," she smiled again.

"Is...Mr. Hendricks here?" Burt decided to go for the jugular.

"Mr. Hendricks owns the business but he is no longer active in the operation...Mr. Cooper has passed on," the girl advised.

"Do you mean...he never comes here?" Burt insisted.

"Mr. Hendricks comes to his office from time to time."

"But he's not here now," Burt pushed.

"He could be in his office... He doesn't check in with me." The girl pressed a tab on her telephone console. "Mr. Acres," she spoke into the headset curled around at her chin. "There is a gentleman here...about television commercials... Yes..." then up to Cummins, "Your name, sir?"

Cummins was caught off guard again... "My name? ... Don't you want her name?" he stalled.

"And her's, too," the girl said.

Burt looked down at the ashtray on the counter...It was empty. "Joe Green" he said suddenly as if he had just remembered, "This is my niece Rita...Randolph."

The blond was back to her phone. "A Mr. Green and a Miss Randolph... Yes, sir, I'll send them right in."

Cummins took a deep breath and turned to face Mary... What danger was he dragging her into now? Once in the office they may have to fight their way out. Burt gave a nervous look to the street. There were no police in sight. The inner office would give them some protection from the police, but he was sure the office would have it's own perils.

"If you'll go through that door," the blond instructed, "Mr. Acres will take care of you."

Burt had taken Mary's arm and started for the indicated door when he turned back to the receptionist.

"Where did you say Mr. Hendricks' office was?"

"He has an office upstairs... Mr. Hendricks also has an office in his home and one in Palm Springs. It's hard to tell in which one he might be at any given time "

"Thank you," said Cummins and continued to the door.

A tall man, prematurely gray, bright eyes smiling out of a sun reddened face, was standing inside with a hand extended in greeting. His broad shoulders fitted into a navy blue blazer with a suffer's patch sewn onto the left breast pocket. An honor most likely earned rather than a designer's 'macho building' adornment. He wore a white turtleneck sweater that corseted any sagging neck muscles he might have had.

"Hello, I'm Paul Acres," the man said in a booming, theatrical voice. "You are Mr. Green? And this must be Miss Randolph." They shook hands all round. "Please sit down," he said, indicating the two chairs by his desk.

Mary was the first to take her seat. Burt Cummins took a moment tc survey the office. There were six other people seated at desks, presumably potential clients, and at each desk a man conducting an interview. Burt noted the demensions of the office seemed to be the same as the building. There was no staircase visible. Up or down. At the far end of the rectangular room were two doors, approximtely eight feet apart. The one on the left marked, LADIES, and the door on the right marked MEN. Cummins followed Mary to his chair.

Paul Acres sat down heavily behind his desk and looked expectantly from Mary to Burt. "Didn't the girl have you fill out our questionnaire?"

"No, she didn't," Burt answered.

The man brought another copy of the questionnaire from his desk drawer:

"There are only a few questions and a full statement of what you may expect from Hendricks & Cooper," Acres began to explain.

Cummins took his handkerchief and wiped at the tricklets of perspiration still forming on his face.

"We are not an agency," the man behind the desk said emphatically. "We do not act as an agency. We cannot, and we do not, guarante your ever getting a part in any movie, television or theatrical. But," he said with his eyes lighting up, "what we do, and do very well, is to prepare you properly so you will be ready when the 'break' comes along... And it will come." He pushed the paper across the desk with a pen along side it...like a closer on a used car lot. "And in paragraph twenty," the man went on, "you will see that we do not charge a commission on any salary you obtain in the industry. Even if you earn into the millions, as many do out here, you will never pay us one cent... only the fees for service and material as stipulated in this contract." He then set the pen on top of the paper.

Burt Cummins' immediate impulse was to ask how a 'questionnaire' could become a contract, but instead, he said, "Mr. Acres, I am only interested in seeing that...Rita has a chance to be in television or the movies... And I'm willing to pay...whatever it takes."

At the words 'pay whatever,' Paul Acres' face registered BINGO. He clasped his hands together and leaned forward in a very confidential manner. "I can't tell you how many, absolutely fine actors, don't get to first base at their auditions and interviews... The reason is they have not learned how to present themselves professionally. How to speak. Voice placement. What to say and what not to say. How to dress, your makeup. How to handle a 'cold reading'... There are so many ways we can help. It won't happen over night, but it will happen and the trick is to be ready when opportunity knocks."

Time was running out and Cummins knew he had to make a move... He wiped his face again... "Excuse me... Do you have a men's room..? I'm not feeling well."

Mary had her right hand in her purse below the level of the desk and was about to take the gun out and slip it to Burt, but the man behind the desk rose from his chair and her move could no longer be hidden.

"At the rear of the office, Mr. Green," Mr. Acres said.

"I only need some cold water on my face... Rita will be able to answer your questions... Excuse me." Cummins went quickly down the isle betwen the desks and into the door at the end of the office marked MEN.

"That was sudden," said Acres sitting down again.

"He...became ill on the plane flying in." Mary wondered if Burt would cross her story when he returned. "Nothing serious, I'm sure." Her hand was still in her purse, her finger on the trigger of the snubnose .38.

Inside the men's room, Burt first noticed that the door opened to the right and a solid wall was immediately to his left...even though there was eight feet between the doors. Perhaps the ladies' room took up that space, or the unaccounted for area concealed a staircase. If so, the entrance was from the parking lot behind the building.

Burt went to the sink against the far wall and ran cold water on his handkerchief. His face was still warm and his desperation was coming to a boil. "If there is a staircase, it might lead upstairs...upstairs to Hendricks' office." Burt was thinking as he wiped his face.

Cummins was starting to wring out his handkerchief when a loud buzz and whirr of an electric motor was heard. It seemed to come from behind the wall where he thought a stairwell might be. The sound grew louder. Metal grinding on metal. Cummins pressed his ear to the wall. The sound was definitely that of an electric motor. A large one. Maybe a wench. Rolling wheels on a track. The sound began at the ceiling and he could follow the rumble as it moved down the wall and passed below the floor into the basement. Was it a dumb waiter in the building? Was it just a motor that had nothing to do with anything? Or...was it an elevator that went from the floor above to the basement, bypassing the main floor? Was this Hendricks' private elevator so he could come and go without being seen by anyone on the first floor? If Cummins was correct in his speculations, Hendricks could be on his way out of the building now...Burt shoved the wet handkerchief in his pocket and almost ran back to where Mary was sitting.

"Rita," Burt pulled her up from the chair by the arm. "We'll have to come back tomorrow...I don't have the time now." Mary was on her feet. "I'm sorry, Mr. Acres. I'll ask for you so you won't lose your commission...Sorry."

Burt held Mary's arm as they went through the door, passed the startled receptionist and out to the sidewalk.

"What did you find?" Mary asked.

"I'm not sure, but I think Hendricks is trying to get out of the building now...around in back...come on."

Burt started running and Mary was trying to keep up with him. "Wait," Mary called. "Here, take the gun."

Burt took the .38 from her.

"What about the keys?" Mary asked.

"The keys?"

"Maybe one of the keys Johnson had is for a door around here."

Burt took both the gun and the keys. Reaching the corner of the building, he put his arm out to keep Mary close to the wall, "Stay back and be careful."

Burt held the gun tightly in his right hand. It felt strange...heavy. The last time he had a gun in his hand was basic training, and that was an Ml. Could he fire the .38 and if he did, could he hit anything?

Slowly he peeked around the corner. There was no door in the rear wall. At the far side was an iron staircase, like a fire escape, attached to the building. The stairs went from ground level of the parking lot to the second floor where there was a recessed doorway.

"Burt," Mary whispred. "Someone is going to see us and call the police."

"They won't have far to drive," Burt said offhand, his attention was on the entrance above his head. "That elevator was going down," he remembered. Then he saw the stairwell. A short set of cement steps going down to a basement door with thin iron bars across a small window in the upper half.

"Mary, you stay here...or better yet, go across the street and wait for me."

"Why can't I go with you?" Mary asked.

"I don't know what's down there, and it's safer alone...Now go. Hurry."

Burt moved around the corner, staying so close to the brick wall that he was tearing his tweed jacket and scraping the skin on the back of his hand on the rough mortar joints. His eyes went first to the landing at the top of the stairs and he saw the telvision camera above the arched doorway. The camera seemed to be moving slowly to the left, away from him. He would have to move before it completed its oscilation and came back toward him...or he could try to make it down the cement steps. The stairwell was directly below the second floor landing and blocked the view of the searching camera.

186

Burt was edging along the wall like a man on a narrow ledge ten stories above the street. The door on the second floor swung open. Burt made a run for it and took the basement steps two at a time till he reached the bottom. He forced himself to the corner of the stairwell, his face against the damp green moss growing on the concrete. The door above was now closing and he could hear someone descending the iron steps. He saw shoes, black leather shoes, then black trousers of a man. For a better view, Burt climbed the steps behind him, backwards, one at a time, until he could see the man's hands. In his right hand he was holding a book, but not a book, it was the size of a book, black and plastic looking...a case of some kind. Burt's eyes were now level with the tarmac of the parking lot. He could see the full figure of a man with his back to him... ''How the hell will I know Hendricks, I've never seen the son-of-a-bitch.'' Cummins' eyes followed the man as he moved into the parking lot and headed for a small car. Then he could see the man's face. ''My God. Professor Hamilton... But it can't be... What the hell is he doing here?'' Burt had no answer, but it was Hamilton, no doubt about it...he was so sure that he was about to call out to his former teacher, but caught himself in time.

In utter disbelief, Cummins watched his trusted friend get into his small car and drive out of the parking lot at a high rate of speed. His mind could not fit this part of the puzzle into the overall picture...''Why?''

Burt moved back down the steps and put his face up to the bars protecting the small dirty window. He could see nothing. He cupped his hands on both sids of his face to shield his eyes from the reflected sunlight. Still he could see nothing. He examined the door. There was no knob, no handle. The lock was high on the left side. Burt took the keys he had taken from Johnson's pocket...there were ten on a steel ring. The long, thin one was for the Datsun. He remembered that. Two keys were very small and obviously not for the lock on this door. One by one he tried the remaining keys in the lock...the seventh key slid in...it fit... Burt's mind told him of the hundreds of keys he had used in his life, keys that would fit into a lock...but would not turn to open it. With the thumb and knuckle of the first finger, he put pressure to the right. The key turned in the lock and the door swung open toward him. Burt reached for the edge of the door and brought it full open. Inside was darkness. One careful step at a time he moved through the doorway and closed the door behind him.

Anyone who would go to the trouble and expense of having a remote television camera mounted on a door would surely have some type of alarm on all other doors. Burt was positive he had just set one off somewhere in the building when he opened the door. He would have to move fast. But where?

Cummins walked further into the basement, his eyes becoming more accustomed to the darkness. He worked his way across the room. Past the sign shop, past the pile of tables and chairs. He turned to see what looked like a cage. An enclosure with walls of cyclone fencing from floor to ceiling. He saw a canvas army cot, a wooden crate, and by the wall a brokendown toilet. "Could this be where they have been holding Martha?" he cried. "Where is she, where is she? Oh, God, help me." His fingers clung to the heavy wire of the fencing.

Cummins forced himself to move. He walked around old boxes, discarded lamps and rugs. Through the dimness he saw a strange configuration of pipes and iron...a giant Erector Set. He moved closer. Now he could see it was the skeleton of an elevator shaft. The square opning in the floor going down to an even darker second basement. Above he could make out the bottom of the elevator with its thick cables and counter weights looping down. On either side of the shaft were two sets of guide rails that came down from the floor above and went into the basement below.

Burt had to find a way to the second floor without going up the outside stairway and into the warning eye of the television camera. Could he chance the elevator and hope for the element of surprise? If he pressed the button, would he reach the top floor alive? His finger was shaking an inch from the 'down' button. Burt Cummins was on his 'trestle' and the freight train was pounding toward him fast.

The sudden rumble of the electric elevator motor, and the noise of the cables, caused Cummins to jerk his hand back from the 'down' button as if his finger had touched a hot wire.

The elevator had started down and the heavy, grease encrusted counter-weights were moving up past his face.

Cummins looked desperately about the basement for a place to hide. The chairs and boxes were too small to afford concealment. The rugs would take too much time to arrange. Fifteen feet to his left he saw a dusty speaker's lectern standing behind a broken table. It was all of four feet high and if he bent down behind it, he would be out of sight.

The elevator was now clearing the main floor and in seconds it would be in the basement.

Reaching the lectern, Cummins saw it was the type that once had its own public address system built-in, the amplifier had been taken out and the twelve inch speaker was gone. A thin, red cloth was stretched over the speaker opening in the front.

Cummins set the briefcase in first, and by dropping to his knees, and stumping forward, he could hide himself inside the empty lectern with only the heels of his shoes exposed at the rear.

The motor noise ended and the elevator came to a rattling stop. The steel folding door was pushed open. Burt could see clearly through the loosely woven material that had been designed to freely transmit sound, while shielding the crude mechanics of the cone-speaker from view.

Burt watched two men come from the elevator.

The basement door must have set off an alarm, Burt was telling himself. These two are looking for the intruder. But their movements belied his suspicion. They walked unhurried and Burt could see no gun. One man reached into his pocket and drew out a set of keys as he passed within five feet of Burt's hiding place. They moved further to his right and, though Burt could see very clearly when looking directly ahead, he found that when the angle became severe, he could see nothing.

Cummins face was against the speaker cloth and he inhaled the accumulated dust into his mouth and nose. He found his lips moving in a silent prayer and he was no longer within the confines of a discarded wooden lectern, but in a small, musty confessional, and he was nine years old. It was the Friday before his First Communion. Sister Mary Bonita had ushered the entire second grade into the empty gray stone church... He sat on the wooden bench, his eyes on the high vaulted ceiling until a stern finger-snap from Sister told him to kneel, and put his face in his hands and to examine his conscience. To list, in his mind, his sins and have the most grievous at the top, then down the list to the less serious...like whispering in class. He was kneeling inside a small, dark wooden closet. His face against the screen at the window. The screen that protects the frightened penitent from the knowing eyes of the priest. The panel slid to the side and Burt could see Father Fox. What little light there was came from a tiny amber overhead bulb. The purple stole was about the priest's neck. Father Fox leaned his head close to the window and began a whispered prayer. The nine year old boy began, "Bless me Father, for I have sinned, my last confession was..." the thin voice of his memory halted. "My last confession was...forty-seven years ago." Burt Cummins was praying. "Dear God... I don't deserve your help. I don't deserve that you should even hear me...but Martha does... You know Martha does... Please let no harm come to her... Please let me help her. Please... Then do with me as you will."

Through a swirl of time, Burt could hear the wooden panel slide closed. He backed out of the lectern carefully and rose just enough to see over the top.

One of the men had taken a key and opened a door. A light was turned on inside a small room. A table was in the center and he could see cardboard boxes piled high against the back wall. From one of the boxes the second man took, what looked like, a book. It was the same as he saw Professor Hamilton carry from the building. These men were opening these 'books,' these small cases, and putting a white packet, about the size of a tea bag, in each. Then the case was snapped closed and put onto a stack. This was repeated until there were two stacks of five.

"That's the end of it." the taller man said.

"Yeah, the boss is going to have a shit hemorrhage. We haven't sent the shipment to Denver and we still have that order for Phoenix," the other man added.

"We've never been this low on the stuff. Only have these ten for the local talent at Diablo Canyon."

"Something must be wrong...Johnson should have been back by now." The man picked up his five cases.

"If Hendricks wants to tell me what's wrong, he'll tell me. I'm not making the mistake of asking him, you can bet your ass on that."

They both laughed and Cummins bent down out of sight behind the lectern.

The light was turned off in the room and the two men carried their cases to the elevator and stepped in. Burt saw the door slide closed and heard the start of the motor and the elevator was on its way up.

Hendricks waited until Miss Phillips had left his office before he went to where Martha Cummins sat on a chair in the center of the room. Her blindfold was still in place and her wrists were bound.

Without warning Hendricks drew his right hand back and slapped Mrs. Cummins with all his strength across her face. The force of the unexpected blow sent her reeling from the chair to the floor, landing on her elbow and hip. She lay on her side, too stunned to move. Only conscious of a dull ringing in her head and the pain building on the left side of her face.

Hendricks moved to the fallen woman and grasped her wrists and roughly pulled her up to her feet and then pushed her down onto the chair.

"I told you I had very little time..." Hendricks was shouting. "If you value your life, and that of your husband, you will tell me the truth... Now. Tell me about your brother's company." He held her shoulders and shook her. "Tell me."

Martha Cummins was still confused. She did not know what this man wanted. Hadn't she told him everything she knew? What more could she tell him?

The swelling had begun on her cheek and lips and when she tried to speak no words would form. Blood ran from the corner of her mouth and a tooth that Hendricks had broken when he slapped her was causing excruciating pain.

Hendricks began shaking Martha again and her head was banging violently against the high back chair.

"Tell me," was his frenzied demand.

"I have told you all I know," Martha Cummins managed to say.

"You have told me lies. All lies," Hendricks was yelling as his frustration mounted.

The flow of blood from the deep cut on Martha's lip and from her torn gum filled her mouth and she was forced to swallow the blood to prevent choking.

"There is no Rocky Mountain Pharmaceutical Company in Las Vegas." Hendricks spit the words out. "My people have gone over every inch of that town and found nothing."

"No, no." The sound came through Martha's bloody and swollen lips. "My brother George... Everyone in town knows him.. He has lived there all his life." Martha fought to get each word out. "His company is one of the biggest in New Mexico."

Hendricks stopped cold. "NEW MEXICO?" His hand was raised to slap her again. "Las Vegas, New Mexico? There is a Las Vegas in New Mexico?"

"Yes, yes, there is. I was born there." Martha sobbed.

Hendricks' eyes were glazed. Had he been tricked? Was Martha Cummins still stalling for time?

"Why didn't you say New Mexico?" Hendricks challenged.

"You didn't give me a chance." Mrs. Cummins wiped the dripping blood from her chin with the sleeve of her blouse.

Hendricks was at his phone pressing the intercom button. "Get Phillips in here... Now." He put the phone down and turned his back on Mrs. Cummins and walked to the high window. Hendricks was still looking for the black Datsun with Arizona plates. "Why hasn't Johnson gotten here?" he asked himself aloud.

When Hendricks heard Miss Phillips come into the office, he half turned from the window. "Take her to the basement." he ordered.

Miss Phillips looked at Martha's bruised face, then gave a smile of approval to Mr. Hendricks. She took Mrs. Cummins by the arm and hurried her from the office.

A very irritated Hendricks continued to watch the traffic flow past his building. When, after ten minutes no black Datsun with Arizona plates had entered his parking lot, he went to his desk and sat down. His clenched fist beating a steady rhythm on the green blotter.

"The hours I have wasted... I could have made new connections in San Salvador or someplace by now... Who the hell do I know in New Mexico?"

The tempo of his pounding fist quickened. ''If Johnson has lost this shipment...or stolen it... I have not only thrown away two million dollars, but more important, I have lost the work that the shipment would do for the cause...'' Both palms came down on the desk, ''Goddamn this bunch of stupid, incompetent Americans I'm forced to work with.''

The phone on his desk buzzed and the intercom light began to flash.

''Yes?''

''Mr. Hendricks, Miss Cook is calling from Phoenix again. She is on line three.''

Without a word Hendricks pressed the line three button.

''Yes, Cook. What is it?''

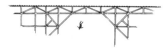

Cummins stayed hidden in the wooden lectern until he heard the elevator come to a stop two floors above the basement. He heard the folding door squeek open and the noise of it slamming shut reverberated down the shaft. The elevator was empty now...quiet. Slowly Cummins backed out of his narrow refuge and stood up. In his right hand was the snubnose .38. He examined it for the first time.

"Why didn't I use it?" Cummins was demanding of himself. "Not to fire the gun or to kill anyone, but to take at least two of Hendricks' men out of the picture." Cummins' hind-sight was now in high gear. "I could have jumped out behind them and yelled, 'STICK 'EM UP'... 'DON'T MOVE I'VE GOT YOU COVERED' or 'FREEZE'... I've seen James Garner do it a hundred times." Instead Cummins had remained hidden until the two men had gone back up to the top floor...and he knew he had only postponed the inevitable confrontation.

Cummins could wait no longer. He had missed his chance to diminish their number by two. He was determined not to let that happen again. Cummins took a tight grip on the .38 and moved to the elevator shaft one more time. His mind was made up. His plan of attack was to take the elevator to the top floor and when the door opened he would challenge whoever might be there. Shoot to kill if need be. Remembering to count the shots. He had only six bullets. They would have to do the job.

Cummins' objective was to find his wife Martha and get her out of the building. If he could find Hendricks in the process.. so much the better. But Martha's safety was his prime concern.

He was about to press the down button with the muzzle of the .38 when the sound of the elevator motor startled him so badly that he fumbled the gun and nearly dropped it. The elevator was coming down. This time it could be Hendricks himself. Cummins decided to retreat to the protection of the lectern. From there he could observe who was in the elevator without being seen.

This time he did not hide inside. He crouched low behind it. His eyes level with the top of the lectern. The .38 up tight by the side of his face.

As the elevator lowered into the basement, Cummins could see two people. Two women. A large woman in a plain green dress. Her right hand gripping the arm of a much smaller woman. They were both facing away from him, but even from the back, Cummins knew instantly the shorter woman was Martha.

Without a beat, Cummins stood full up. The gun now level and pointed at the back of the woman in green.

Phillips slid the door open with her left hand and pushed Martha from the elevator away from Cummins and toward the wire cage. Cummins came around the lectern, walking carefully and moved up on them, closing the separation at a pace that would put him directly behind Phillips when she opened the cage door.

Phillips gave her prisoner a powerful shove causing Martha to stumble and fall against the far wall of the room.

Cummins took one more step and pressed his gun to Phillips' neck. "You make one move lady, and I'll blow your head off."

The woman in green did not make one move. She made three lightening fast moves. First, her right elbow whistled back digging into Cummins' chest with such force it doubled his arms in front of him. Her second move drove the flat of her hand in a karate chop under his right ear. The third move was a wrist lock on his gun hand delivering such pain it forced his fingers open and the .38 dropped to the floor. Cummins helplessly watched the woman kick the gun away. He was now bent almost double and Phillips clasped both her hands and brought them down on the back of his neck driving him to his knees. She then grabbed a handful of Cummins' hair and forced his head back and she sent her right knee slamming into his up-turned chin, snapping his teeth together. Cummins was thrown back against the wire wall of the cage. He had lost all control of his arms and legs, a rag doll in a dream where you try to run and your legs will not respond to the commands of the brain. He slumped to the floor on his side, his face in the dirt of the cement. The woman was coming at him and he could not move to protect himself. She drove her foot deep into the pit of his stomach and had drawn back to kick him a second time when he found the strength to catch her foot with both hands and twist the ankle a full turn. Phillips, rather than have an ankle broken, gave way and spiraled to the floor. Cummins crawled over her fallen body and began hitting her in the face. His fists had no coordination or power. His punches were uncontrolled, his arms rubbery. Phillips' arms were flailing at Cummins, easily fending off his meager blows. Her hands found Cummins' throat and clamped on. Her powerful fingers squeezed his windpipe. Her clawlike fingernails dug into the flesh of his neck.

Cummins tried to free himself by tugging at her strong arms, but her pressure grew tighter. He knew that a few more seconds would render him unconscious. With a desperate lurch, Cummins braced himself by holding both Phillips' wrists and throwing his body high into the air and coming down on her stomach with both his knees. Phillips gave a grunt and was forced to release her hold and roll to her side, letting Cummins drop to the floor. She then scrambled awkwardly to her hands and knees and crawled toward the gun that had slid under the canvas cot. Cummins saw her intention and rose to his feet and with two running steps leaped on her back, forcing her to crash into the wooden edge of the cot and their combined weight breaking the legs and causing the cot to collapse. The side rail pinned Phillips' wrist to the floor, the gun inches from her outstretched fingers. She was an animal in a sprung trap. Her heavy body tossing from side to side in an attempt to throw Cummins from her back. She reached with all her strength, ripping the skin from the back of her hand as she struggled to get a finger around the triggr of the .38. Cummins knew that a shot would bring everyone in the building down to the basement. He must not let her reach that gun.

Then for the first time, Cummins saw his wife. Her swollen and bloody face, the cruel blindfold and bound wrists. He wanted to cry out. He pressed down with all his weight on Phillips' wrist, but her hand was inching closer to the .38. For a split second Cummins saw the wine bottle on the wooden box next to the broken cot. His arm made a wide swing catching the neck of the bottle in his right hand and with the same movement he brought the bottle down on the woman's head. Her body stiffened and shook for a moment, then was still. Cummins held the bottle high over his head ready for a second blow if necessary, but her body lay motionless.

Cummins reached over and picked up the gun and quickly moved to where Martha was sitting on the floor with her fingers clinging to the cyclone fencing and her face pressed against the wire.

"Martha, my darling," Burt put his arms around his wife and kissed her head. "What have they done to you?"

Martha fought off the torment of her darkness. "Burt?" Blood was still heavy in her mouth. "Burt, is that you?"

"Yes, darling. Yes, it's me."

"Burt...thank God you're here..." Martha was crying. "How did you find me?"

Cummins took her hands and began to unwind the tape from her wrists. "Martha, darling, you're alright now. You are safe now."

When Burt had freed Martha's wrists, he began to unwind the tape from her eyes. "They can't hurt you now..." Burt was saying as he carefully removed the last of the bandage.

Martha, with the bandage off, could not open her eyes. After two days the white adhesive material of the bandage had caked on her eyelids and lashes and she had to peal away the hardened substance.

"Burt," Martha was forcing the words. "These people are insane. They wanted you and then they said if I didn't tell them where my brother George was, they would kill me..." Again her voice fought back hysteria.

"Can you walk?" Burt was lifting her to her feet. "I have to get you out of here."

"Why do they want to hurt George? Why?"

"They don't want George. They want me. But that's all over with now." Burt had one arm around Martha's waist and she was holding on to his shoulder.

They moved out of the wire cage and across the basement, past the elevator and found their way to the basement door at the rear of the building.

The afternoon sky was bright and Martha covered her eyes to protect them from the sun's glare.

Halfway up the basement steps, Burt saw two police cars in the rear parking lot. He stopped and pulled Martha back down two steps.

"What is it Burt? What is it?" His sudden move had been so unexpected, Martha began to shake.

Burt had his arm around his wife and was holding her from continuing up the steps. "Martha, do you think you can make it up these stairs and over to the police car? Do you think you can do it?"

"I think so, but why?"

"I have to go back in there... Something I have to do." Burt looked over the edge to see if the men around the police car had moved.

"I'll try Burt... Why can't you come with me?" Her hands tightened on his arm.

"Stay here and count to fifty...then go up the stairs and walk over to the police... Tell them to wait by the door at the top of those iron steps." Burt gave his wife a kiss on her tearfilled eyes. "This is very important... Can you do it?" Burt was already reaching for the key that would open the basement door.

"Please be careful," said Martha.

"Be sure to count to fifty, slowly, before you go to the police."

Burt did not wait for an answer. He was down the steps and opening the steel door. He moved inside going directly to the elevator shaft and pushed the 'down' button and it seemed that the motor started a fraction of a second before he had depressed the button. He wasn't sure. The elevator was coming down. It was then he remembered the elevator was in the basement when he and Martha walked by it a minute ago. Someone had brought the elevator back up...and now it was on it's way down. Cummins backed a few feet into the darkness... As the elevator came into view he could see it carried the two men he had seen in the basement a short while ago. The elevator stopped and the taller man slid the door open. At that moment he saw Phillips on the floor of the cage and they both started for the door.

"Hold it right there." Cummins ordered, his gun pointed at them as he moved forward.

The two men turned with their arms held away from their bodies.

"Drop your guns on the floor... Now." Burt moved a step closer.

The taller man took a gun from his belt using his thumb and first finger. The gun fell to the floor.

"I don't have a gun," the second man said as he raised his hands higher.

Cummins put his .38 in the man's face. "O.K. I'll shoot you, then I'll search you."

The man raised the flap of his jacket and turned part way around. Burt reached out and took a gun from the man's belt in the center of his back. He tossed the gun into the darkness of the basement.

"Into the cage with your friend... Move."

The two man went into the wire cage as Burt pulled the door closed and set the lock... The full realization of what he was doing still was not getting to him.

He had the three of them in the cage and the door locked... But he had inadvertently left the key to the lock in the cage with them.

"Shit." said Cummins when he realized what he had done.

There was no way he could reenter the cage and retrieve the key. He was holding the gun on the two men who stood motionless facing him through the cyclone fencing, their hands held up even with their shoulders. Cummins was sure the woman, who was unconscious on the floor, had the key... It was in her pocket, or on her belt, or her wrist; it was somewhere, and in time they would find it, free themselves and be after him.

Cummins moved to the lecturn for the briefcase, then ran to the elevator. Once inside, he turned to see the two man had not moved. Cummins pressed the 'up' button. There was no sound. The elevator did not start. He pressed the button a second time. Still the elevator would not move. He pressed again and again.

"To hell with it," Cummins growled in disgust and a creeping hint of relief... "I'll let the police take care of Hendricks."

As the thoughts were forming, Cummins recognized the pattern. Instant rationalization to accommodate his phobia. "It's not my fault the damn elevator won't start... Haven't I done all I can? Martha is safe. What more is there? The police are paid to take risks, I'm not." The distant chant from a dark corner of his memory began, "SCAREDY-CAT - SCAAREDY-CAT...CUMMINS IS A SCAREDY-CAT..." Once again he would be turning his back and running. But running away was easy now. He had done it so many times in his life, the action was not only automatic, but completely tolerable and appropriate to the present situation.

Amid the jungle of justificatory thoughts, the aggravating question was clawing it's way to the surface of his brain... "Must I carry that haunting chant of those kids the rest of my life."

"NO." Cummins shouted. "Goddamn it. Not this time."

Cummins backed into the elevator and pressed the 'up' button hard. He pressed it again and held it. The elevator did not move. He looked at the two men in the cage. Their hands seemed to have lowered ever so slightly. Then he saw that he had not closed the folding door. With one pull he slammed it shut, pressed the button and the elevator started up.

Cummins bent down to keep the two men in sight until the floor of the elevator cleared the basement ceiling. With one inch of clearance he saw the two men start for the woman on the floor in search of the key, then they were out of sight.

Now, in seconds, he would be putting into action the plans he had formulated. When the elevator stopped, he would open the door and challenge whoever might be there and he would shoot if he had to.

The elevator came to a bouncing stop.

Cummins slid the folding door to one side and opened the half glass door to the office. The office was empty and silent. He looked to the left and to the right. Before him was a desk and an empty chair behind it. Cummins reached back to close the door, then suddenly stopped.

"If the elevator would not operate with the door open for me...I will leave the door open and the two men will not be able to bring it down, even if they find the key and open the lock."

Cummins had little time to savor his brilliant decision. As he moved across the reception room, Cummins saw two unmarked doors. Which one would be Hendricks'... He began to move forward when a small noise stopped him... Metal on metal. Like a tin door closing. Cummins turned in the direction of the sound. He had taken only two steps when he heard it again. This time louder...pernaps not louder but nearer. It was coming from a hallway to his right. A rolling sound of metal wheels, then a closing door sound. As he gained the corner he saw a woman opening a large filing cabinet. Her back was to Cummins and she did not know he was behind her until he pressed his gun to her back and whispered:

"Don't make a sound."

The woman did not turn or make any sound. She stood in front of an open file drawer with several manila folders in her hands.

"Put the papers down, lady, and turn around...slowly."

The woman did as she was told. As she turned, Cummins saw she was in her forties or more. Her jet-black hair was obviously a wig. Her oval face and expressive eyes told you she had at one time been a person of great beauty. Now her deep, sunken eyes were bloodshot and recent tears had left rivulets of mascara down both cheeks.

"I don't want to hurt you," Cummins said, holding the gun to her chest. "I want Hendricks. Where is he?"

The lady took time to compose herself, then she said, "In his office."

"Which ofice? Which door?" Cummins questioned.

The lady pointed over his shoulder, "The second door, on the left."

Cummins took a step back and motioned for the woman to move by him to her desk.

She moved quickly and sat down, her hands folded in her lap...her eyes looking at the floor.

Cummins was now at a loss as to how he could keep her there. He saw nothing in the office to tie her with...and once he moved away from her she could scream a warning.

In desperation, he said, ''The elevator. Get in the elevator. Hurry.''

The woman rose from her chair and went to the elevator door which Cummins was holding open for her.

One step from the door she stopped.

''You are Doctor Cummins, aren't you?''

Cummins gave no answer.

''I'm very sorry about your wife...really I am. There was nothing I could do.''

Cummins was about to speak, but instead he motioned her into the elevator with the gun.

''You go to the basement, and if you are smart, you will continue right out the back door...'' Cummins slid the folding door closed, then warned. ''If anyone comes up this elevator, I'll kill them.''

The woman pressed the down button and Cummins closed the outer door and watched the shadow move down the frosted glass panel of the door. He then turned and walked across the office toward the second door on the left, as directed by the tearful lady.

At the second door, Cummins stopped to listen. There was no sound inside. Had the lady tricked him? Would he be walking into a trap? He put his hand on the knob and turned slowly. There was a light click and the door was open. He pressed forward and the door gave inward one inch. He could see a large chair, then a desk. He opened the door far enough to allow his head to get in. There, standing, looking out the window with his back to him, was Hendricks. A tall, powerfully built man, with broad shoulders and a head set on a thick, bull of a neck. The 38 felt reassuring in Cummins hand. He would be no match for this man, hand to hand. The woman in the basement proved that.

Cummins closed the door behind him hard enough for it to be heard. Hendricks was still looking out the window and began to speak before turning around.

''Mrs. Cooper, did you get the...'' Hendricks left his question hanging as he froze momentarily, his eyes caught on the 38 in Cummins' hand. He then bolted across the room in an attempt to reach his desk. Cummins intercepted him with his gun at Hendricks' ear.

''Move again and I'll put a bullet through your head.'' Cummins held the gun steady while Hendricks straightened up and stepped back from the desk.

Cummins backed away to give himself some distance between them. "Is this what you have been looking for?" and he threw the briefcase on the floor at Hendricks' feet.

Hendricks looked down at the brown leather case, knowing what it held inside and knowing how important those three plastic bags were to his plans. His eyes moved up to meet Cummins'.

Cummins went behind Hendricks' desk and opened the top center drawer and brought out a .45 semi-automatic. As he placed Hendricks' gun in his belt, he noticed how much larger and heavier it was, and he hoped it would not slip down into his pants.

"Sit down, Mr. Hendricks and put your hands on the desk."

Cummins watched as Hendricks went behind the desk and sank into his chair.

"Mr. Hendricks, I'm Burton Cummins."

"I know."

"What you don't know is that I am going to kill you. First, I am going to beat your face in for what you did to my wife, then I am going to put this gun in your mouth and blow your Goddamn head off."

Hendricks studied Cummins for what seemed like minutes.

"No, Doctor. You will not kill me... Not you. You can't." Hendricks' words had an hypnotic texture in their delivery.

"I can't?" Cummins asked. "What about Faber...and Johnson? What makes you think for a second I wouldn't kill you?"

"Faber and Johnson...that was differnt. If indeed you did kill them, it was in hot blood...as opposed to cold blood...like now."

"You just try me, Mr. Hendricks... After what you did to my wife I could kill you and really enjoy it." Cummins paused. "I never thought I could say that, but it's true. I will enjoy seeing you die."

"Revenge is sweet, but I have something sweeter."

Hendricks made a small move with his right hand. "May I show you something? I think you will be interested in this. I'll have to open this drawer."

Cummins was letting Hendricks talk too much. If he was going to do what he came up to do, he should get on with it, but he said, "Be very careful."

Hendricks pulled out the top right drawer, using his thumb and first finger. He then reached in and brought out four bound stacks of hundred dollar bills and dropped them on the top of the desk.

"There is five hundred thousand dollars...a half million...and it can be yours. You take the money and leave the case with me." Both men eyed each other. "Isn't that what you asked for on the phone...almost that much..." Hendricks flipped over the stacks of bills so they were side by side. "Do we have a deal?"

Cummins stood watching Hendricks, his hand holding the gun was wet with sweat. He moved closer to the desk and touched each stack of hundred dollar bills.

"And you believe this half million is payment enough for the anguish and pain you caused my wife. You really believe money will pay back for the misery you put that woman through?"

"You want more? ...I'll ante up another two hundred thousand."

Cummins leaped forward and struck Hendricks' hand against the drawer and closed it on his wrist.

"Alright," said Hendricks. "Look for yourself... Go ahead... There is two hundred thousand in that drawer... No gun, no knife... just money."

Hendricks moved back in his chair and Cummins pulled the drawer open, keeping the gun in Hendricks' face. His fingers were groping in the shallow drawer until he touched the stack of bills. He drew it out and threw it on the desk.

"See," said Hendricks with a smile. "Now do we have a deal?"

"What makes you think I won't kill you, take the money and the coke?" Cummins demanded.

Hendricks folded his fingers across his chest and gave Cummins the smile of a forgiving father... "She won't let you." And his head gave a nod, to indicate someone behind him.

Cummins did not move. This was a trick. He had seen James Garner in films... The bad guy says, 'Look behind you'... Garner looked and the bad guy jumped him... He wasn't going to go for that old trick.

"There is nobody behind me, Mr. Hendricks."

"Yes, there is, Doctor... Right behind you."

Cummins hadn't heard her come into the office. He turned to see the woman from the filing cabinet. The thin lady who said she was sorry for what had happened to Martha Cummins. Now she stood in the office, pointing a chrome plated revolver.

Hendricks made a move at Cummins to take his gun.

"Hold it." said Mrs. Cooper, and she advanced past Cummins and confronted Hendricks with her gun pointed at his heart.

"What are you doing?" Hendricks yelled as he was forced back into his chair, more afraid for his life than when confronted by Cummins. "What are you doing?"

204

"Something I should have done long ago...I should have killed you the night Paul died... The night he was murdered." Mrs. Cooper was breathing like she had just run a mile up hill.

"Your husband was killed in an accident...you know that. The police said so."

"After you made it look like an accident... And God forgive me, I helped you... I helped you. You thought I was too high to remember... I remember. You said Paul had killed himself and the insurance wouldn't pay of on suicide... We made his murder look like an accident. We."

"You got your money, didn't you...every penny of it." Hendricks made a move to rise, as if he had turned the lady's mind around at the mention of money. Using money to stall for time, as he had done so successfully with Cummins.

"I got the money...and in a month you had it all. You and your Goddamn 'happy dust,' you got me strung out, then you made me pay...with my money...then my body..."

"It wasn't the first time you paid with your body... And you loved it." If Hendricks could keep her talking... Cummins was watching a master mind-bender at work.

"And you never let me forget that...did you? Always threatening to tell Paul he married a hooker... Well, I loved Paul and I was a good wife to him..."

"Look here," Hendricks motioned to the stacks of bills on his desk. "Over a half million dollars... Take what you want... I never wanted your money... and in that briefcase we have enough..."

"In that briefcase," Mrs. Cooper cut him off, "you have enough cocaine to get your sick message into a hundred movies and television shows, oral pornography on records. You have enough in that case to twist the minds of millions of young kids... I'm not going to let you do it anymore."

"You know I don't sell to kids... You know that." Hendricks was back in his chair.

"You don't sell to kids because they don't have the money... That shit cost five times more than gold. No...you don't sell to kids... You sell, even give away, to those that have the most influence on the kid's mind... that's what you're after, isn't it? Their minds."

"For God's sake, put that gun away and take the money and the briefcase." Hendricks made a move to rise. Like it was all settled ...finished...he had won. Cummins watched Mrs. Cooper.

"We made Paul's death look like an accident... I want everyone to know your death was no accident... I want everyone to know that I killed you... I rid the world of scum that walked like a man.''

Hendricks made a leap from his chair toward the woman. Four shots in quick succession tore through the office. The first shot hitting Hendricks in the face and tearing his nose and cheek and eye away. The other three found targets in his chest and stomach. Hendricks fell back and his weight carried him over the arm of his chair and onto the floor. Blood flowing through his black beard and on to his white shirt.

Cummins moved toward Mrs. Cooper.

She turned hard on him, ''Stay away from me,'' she warned.

Cummins could do nothing but look at the scene before him. Hendricks on the floor behind his desk...half his head blown away. Blood pouring from his chest... The gun in Cummins' hand hung useless and unnoticed...no longer a threat.

''I had to do it... Do you understand? I had to do it...'' Mrs. Cooper was crying and the gun in her hand was shaking. ''That pig...he murdered my husband to get control of the company...and I helped him...half the business wasn't enough...oh, no...he wanted it all...and I helped him get it...I helped him make slaves of hundreds of people...he ran their lives...he got them hooked like he did me...I was a user...but he made me an addict...a crawl-the-wall addict...once you get to that stage, he could do anything he wanted to you.''

Cummins made an attempt to reason with her.

''Mrs. Cooper, I'm a doctor...I can help you.''

Mrs. Cooper backed away from Cummins.

''I told you I was sorry for what he did to your wife...I knew you would kill him...you had every right to want him dead... But if I let you kill him for me...he would have ruined you too. Even in death...he would have ruined your life. So, you see, not just for your wife, not just for me...but for the thousands of lives he has smashed...I had to stop him... You understand, don't you doctor?''

Cummins tried one more time to calm her, to talk to her and to take the gun from her. He moved toward her.

''Stay away. Stay away from me. I don't want to hurt you, I don't want to hurt anyone. I want away from all this.'' She was screaming now, and she ran toward Cummins and he put his arms out to catch her but she evaded his grasp and ran headfirst through the tall window, falling silently to the street below with only the noise of shattered glass hitting the sidewalk.

Cummins moved to the window and forced himself to look down into the street. The body of Mrs. Cooper lay face down on the gray cement, the sun reflecting a halo of spectrumed light on the pieses of glass around her.

Immediately people circled the body. Some were looking up to see Cummins framed by the broken window. One man pointed and shouted, "There he is...I saw him push her." Others looked up.

Cummins moved back into the room. The air was heavy with the smell of gunpower. The body of Hendricks had lost more blood and the rug and walls were splattered red.

On the desk, in front of him were the six packs of hundred dollar billls...on the rug in front of the desk was the brown leather briefcase. Cummins stood in the center of it all, the gun still in his hand. His mind trying to bring it all back together... "That brave lady." was all Cummins could say. "That poor, miserable, brave..."

He did not hear the door burst open behind him. Three uniformed policemen came into the room. Guns drawn. Holding their pistols at arm's length with both hands in front of them pointing at Cummins. "Drop it." one officer commanded.

Cummins let the gun fall to the floor. A second policeman took the .45 from his belt. "Put your arms behind you." he said and the third clasped the handcuffs on his wrists, then patted him from armpit to ankle in search of other weapons.

One officer went behind the desk. "Holy shit... He really blew this one away."

"Look at this," another policeman said, referring to the stacks of bills on the desk. "Somebody is lucky I didn't come in here alone." He laughed but cursed his luck.

A policeman had just finished going through all of Cummins' pockets when two detectives entered the office. The officer handed all he had gathered to the detective.

"Did you read the card?" asked the second detective?

"I was just going to." said the policeman and he read Cummins his rights.

While the card was being read, a detective took the .45 from the officer and picked up the gun from the floor with a pencil through the trigger guard. He put his nose to both muzzles.

"Neither one of these has been fired in months."

The detective walked up to Cummins, "What the hell went on here?"

"It will be difficult to explain," Cummins said simply.

"Well, sir, you Goddamn better be able to explain it and explain it so I can understand it...and you better start now." The detective was nose to nose with Cummins.

The door opened again and another detective entered the room and behind him was Vince Reed, the D.E.A. man from Phoenix, his red walrus mustache and 'I Got'Cha' glint in his eyes.

"Hello, Doctor," was Reed's greeting. Then looking about the room. "I seem to have missed a lot. Will you fill me in?"

"What you are after is in that briefcase on the floor...three bags full... How it got there is a long story."

"I know most of it now. Your wife told me... By the way, we sent her to emergency at Wacker... Just to be sure."

"Thanks."

"And as Paul Harvey says," Reed continued, "I got 'the rest of the story' from your friend, Mary Parker."

"Whatever she did back in Phoenix was to save me, and that guy in the pool, he tried to rape her...it was self-defense but at the time, I was afraid to say anything to you or to anybody."

"That's how they operate. Fear and greed. They know how to use both." The D.E.A. man looked at the pile of bills on the desk. "They sure have the money to throw around."

"Over a half million," Cummins offered.

"What happened to Hendricks?" Reed asked.

"She shot him," Cummins indicated the broken window. "Mrs. Cooper shot him. I wanted to. I came up here to kill him...but I couldn't...she did it for me."

The D.E.A. man moved away and spoke to the other detective in low tones. After a short exchange, he came back to Cummins. "We'll have more questions to ask later... You won't be leaving town...will you?"

Cummins shook his head slowly.

"And Miss Parker. I can reach her through your office?"

Cummins nodded his head.

"We have a real mess to clean up here," then suddenly. "I'm sorry doctor," turning to the police officer behind Cummins, "Take off those handcuffs."

When the cuffs were off, Cummins began to rub his wrists. Reed was handing back his wallet. "Handcuffs are a most degrading thing to have on...I'm sorry." Then he studied Cummins' face. "Hendricks offered you all that cash and you didn't go for it... You are some sort of a special person. Real class. Not too smart sometimes, but you got class... By the way. That Mary Parker. She's got class and then some... She is waiting for you in my car in the parking lot.''

"I'm free to go?'' asked Cummins.

"Sure... And we found those three you locked in the basement... Saved us a lot of work.''

Cummins nodded his thanks and after one final look around the office...the broken window, Hendricks on the floor behind the desk, the brown leather briefcase on the floor and the half million on the desk ... he turned and left the office.

When he was half way down the iron stairweay, at the back of the building, he saw Mary getting out of the D.E.A. man's car and run to meet him. She threw her arms around Cummins and was crying, crying tears of joy.

"Oh, Burt, I was so worried... I heard the shots and then that poor woman coming through that window... I ran to the back here and the police stopped me. I told him everything... I hope I did right.'' Mary was crying and holding onto him. Then she backed away to arm's length. "The man said your wife was taken to the hospital for a checkup... You better get over there.''

"I will...I will in a moment.'' He took her arm and walked her to the white Mark VI... "I have to talk to you...please get in.''

Mary sat in the car and Cummins walked around and got in the driver's side. He did not start the engine but sat facing forward with both hands on the wheel.

"Mary, I have to tell someone...I have to tell you most of all...'' Cummins took his time to arrange his thoughts. "When I went into Hendricks' office...I was going to shoot him...I meant to kill him. But I lost my nerve.''

"You are not a killer,'' Mary assured him. "What's wrong with that?''

"Don't you understand, I wanted to and I couldn't.'' Cummins' hands were working the steering wheel. "And there is something else...Hendricks offered me a half million dollars to just walk away...it was on the top of his desk in hundred dollar bills...a half million.''

"You didn't take it,'' said Mary, "You didn't walk...''

"No, but I thought about it...I thought about it good.''

"But Burt...You did not take the money.''

"Maybe the reason I didn't take the money was because Mrs. Cooper came into the office... She had the guts...she had the guts I didn't have... That little woman shot that dirty son-of-a-bitch... My God, did he have it coming... The things he had done to that poor woman's life... Then to kill herself like that... I'm sick."

Mary put her arm around Burt's shoulder.

"And I've put you through seven kinds of hell in these last days... I'm sorry, Mary."

"I'll live."

Cummins started the car. "I had better go by the hospital and see Martha...it is only a few blocks. You can drop me there and you can take the car and go home or where ever...get some rest."

"I could use a few hours in a hot tub," Mary smiled. Then, "That Mr. Reed. The one who was in Phoenix. He was very understanding. I told him about the man busting into my room and how I hit him with the banderillas, about hitting Johnson with the brick...even why they found your prints on Johnson's shoes."

"My Prints?" said Cummins. "He said I wasn't very smart."

"And Mr. Reed said that when this was all cleared up, he would like to take me out to eat...I think he meant dinner." Mary teased.

"Don't be too sure."

The Mark VI pulled into the emergency entrance at Wacker General Hospital. Burt Cummins turned to face Mary.

"I have been trying to live the life of a thirty-year old swinger... Hell, I'm twenty years past that and then some. I found it's no good trying to be something you're not. You made me feel like I could climb mountains and fight tigers with my bare hands...I thank you for that feeling. They say you can't go back... I think they are right. I can't go back. I found that out. So what I am trying to say is that...this may have started out as a cheap fling...but it became more than that...much, much more. I am...truly very, very fond of you... and it could easily get out of hand. So, when Martha is able to travel, I want to take a long vacation... Maybe go back to a little town in Michigan. There are a few things I want to see again...Mary...do you understand?"

"Yes, Burt, I do. I understand very well and I am proud of you. I am proud of what you are," and Mary leaned over and kissed him lightly on the cheek.

Cummins opened his door and stepped out.

"Use the car for as long as you want. You can leave it at the office. And you know you have your job for as long as you want it, too. I mean that."

"Thanks, Burt."

"For as long as you want," Cummins said again.

"Good bye Burt... Love ya," and the tears began.

Cummins stood back and watched the white Lincoln glide down the driveway and into the street.

"Good bye, Mary," Cummins called as the car sped away.

In the hospital Burt Cummins walked up to the receptionist counter.

"May I see Martha Cummins? I'm her husband."

"Yes, Mr. Cummins," the lady answered. "Mrs. Cummins is out of emergency and they took her to her room. That is room 212."

"It figures."

And Dr. Burton Cummins went upstairs to be with his wife.

THE END

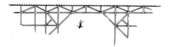

EPILOGUE

There is no proveable correlation connecting the events that followed, but after the death of J.M. Hendricks and the dismantling of his propaganda machine, Frank Swertling wrote the HOLLYWOOD COCAINE CONNECTION for TV Guide. Paul W. Greenberg, executive producer for NBC Nightly News, said Brian Ross and Ira Silverman would continue to pursue the story that cocaine was now a 'second currency in Hollywood' and the favors that currency could buy.

From some mysterious source the United States found there were millions of gallons of gasoline in storage and the OPEC nations were forced to lower the price of their oil. Gasoline went down and American automobiles were once again being built and men and women were going back to work. Inflation leveled off, then fell, and interest rates followed. People were building and buying homes and the stock market hit an all time high of over eleven. The Palo Verde Nuclear Power plant was completed...and Dr. Burton Cummins never saw Mary Parker again...nor his 1983 white Mark VI Lincoln...